RICK L. CAMPISE

LOST MAPLES

A TEXAS WESTERN

Black Rose Writing | Texas

ISBN: 978-1-68433-876-4
PUBLISHED BY BLACK ROSE WRITING
www.blackrosewriting.com

Printed in the United States of America
Suggested Retail Price (SRP) $18.95

Lost Maples is printed in Calluna

*As a planet-friendly publisher, Black Rose Writing does its best to eliminate unnecessary waste to reduce paper usage and energy costs, while never compromising the reading experience. As a result, the final word count vs. page count may not meet common expectations.

This book is dedicated to my grandmother, Rosa "Ma" Eldridge, who introduced me to Louis L'Amour, Zane Grey, Luke Short, and Max Brand novels when I was twelve years old. I have fond memories of sitting in Ma's living room in Somerville, Texas, a fan in the corner swirling heavy Texas heat back and forth, our hands holding worn paperbacks as moist fingertips turned battered pages where heroes emerged to challenge injustice. Those shared summer days in the 1960s were the definition of happiness.

Eternal gratitude to my wife Tib for giving me the time and space to write. Thanks to Reagan Rothe and Black Rose Writing for publishing my first novel.

LOST MAPLES

CHAPTER ONE

The circling hawk saved my life.

Clawing my way through a cloud of pain, I slowly became aware I was laying with my face pressed into the earth, my left nostril producing a small puff of dust with each jagged breath. I was uncertain how long I had been stretched out across the uncomfortable ground, but the chill in my bones indicated I had been laying on the sand and gravel long enough for the cold ground to steal the warmth from my body.

My last memory was shifting my head up and to the left to track the flight of a hawk. This sudden attention to the hawk's flight saved my life. Without that motion, the bullet would have hit dead center in the back of my head. Instead, I had a headache and a bullet burn rather than a hole in my skull.

I could taste the dirt as it swirled around my face. Each breath produced a small cloud of fine grit that settled on my eyelids, lips, and left cheek. The stale dust tasted old and lifeless.

Without moving my head, my eyes tried to focus on something beyond the dirt two inches from my face. Rolling my eyes to the left, I made out a ten-foot by two-foot slice of sunlight on the earth six feet to the left from where I lay. A small painful upward turn of my head revealed the sunlight originated from a similar-sized opening twenty feet in the air.

When shot, I fell off my horse, rolled several feet, and fell in a crack just wide enough that at a perfect angle my body passed through the roof of a cave. I dropped twenty feet and hit an inclined floor that allowed my body to roll away from the opening and into the dark. The floor's slope was the second event that saved my life, my lucky day. If my body had remained visible where it had fallen, I suspect the ambusher would have repeatedly shot into my still form.

The hidden gunman had not followed me down that narrow crevice into the pitch-black void. I could understand why. You could not be certain how far down the blackness extended, and the question remained as to whether you could escape. With a grunt, I lifted my head and was greeted with a wave of nausea that caused me to pass out.

At some point, I awoke and again struggled to get my bearings. Scattered pieces of information floated inside my head as disconnected thoughts. Rubbing my forehead, I remembered it was December of 1839, and I had fallen into a cave after being shot. Fortunately for me, leaves, sticks, and other debris had fallen through the crack in the ceiling. The haphazardly piled debris created a painful, but not deadly cushion when my fall ended on the cave floor.

With the realization my narrow band of sunlight was growing smaller, a sudden panic at being left in complete darkness prompted me into action. Groggily I sat up and moved as far as possible from the opening overhead. I took one of the paper cartridges from a pouch around my waist, tore the end with my teeth, and poured the gunpowder on a small pile of leaves. Piling twigs and small sticks in the center, I built a pyramid of small to medium-sized sticks. Striking my knife on a small stone, the spark hit the gunpowder, the burst of white melting the darkness as the welcome light spread. Despite my circumstances, I smiled. Warmth and light are reassuring when you have been swallowed by darkness.

I checked my Colt Paterson to make sure all five chambers still contained the precious paper cartridges. Holding the pistol in my hand was comforting. I was especially fond of my Colt. Some people viewed guns as cold, deadly pieces of metal. My Colt was a living, breathing, extension of myself.

Though guns existed that could get off more than one shot, the 1836 Colt Paterson was the first mass-produced pistol where a revolving cylinder rotated around a barrel that did not move.[1] My 1839 Colt was the .36 caliber model, a version many people were starting to refer to as the Texas Paterson. With a reloading lever and a capping window, reloads were mercifully shorter.[2] The two-and-a-half-pound pistol felt like it had been made for my hand. With my old friend, I could hit targets at sixty-five yards but was much more comfortable at half that distance.

Reaching for a stick, I heard a rattle and felt a snake strike the heel of my boot. With a quick upper body twist, I turned and shot the head off the biggest rattlesnake I have ever seen. The headless diamondback thrashing violently on the floor was as thick as my wrist and at least seven feet long.

Normally I would not kill a rattler, but he started the fight. On top of that, this rattlesnake was one long piece of meat and I had not eaten in two days.

Concerned there might be other snakes in the cave, I carefully reached down, picked up a stick, and began to weave other sticks and twigs around the tip as a crude torch. When I dipped the torch into the fire it lit up immediately.

Waving the torch in the dim light, I began to make out objects. The narrow crack I had fallen through was two feet from a smooth wall that reached from the floor to the ceiling. A close examination with the torch revealed the smoothness offered no hand or footholds for climbing to the crack twenty feet above my head. From where I stood, there was just deep blackness reaching out in the other three directions.

Though I could not see it, I could smell and hear the slow drip of water. Readily available water was critical if I wanted to get out of this situation alive. For the moment, I was set with water, fire, and food courtesy of the ill-tempered rattler.

Holding the torch aloof, I swept it left to right peering intently through the darkness. In the flickering light, my eyes followed the slow sweep of the torch. I was jolted as an image my eyes had quickly passed over suddenly registered in my mind. A figure sat in the dark staring at me.

Passing the torch to my left hand, I grabbed my pistol with my right hand while pointing the torch where my brain had recognized the shape of a sitting man in the dim cave. I was not alone. In the grey light, I could see a figure wearing a battered hat, a cow skin jacket, tattered pants, and badly scuffed miner boots. Against the stone wall sat a long-dead man whose skeleton was held together by his clothes.

For the longest time, I simply stared at the figure, half expecting him to get up and move toward me. I crouched down on my heels and from a distance studied every aspect of the dead figure. Had he been shot? Did he fall through the crack? Was I to be imprisoned in the cave until my death too?

I noted a battered hat was tilted over his face, or at least I assumed it was a face, it might be a skull precariously sitting on the collar of his jacket. One pants leg was ripped from the ankle to the knee and a bone jutted out unnaturally.

The dead man's bony hand appeared to be clutching a fragment of paper yellowed with age. I reached over and delicately removed the crumpled paper. The painfully scribbled words read *Damn rattler bit me. Fell and broke my leg. You can have the gold on two conditions, 1-Kill the snake, 2-I like sitting here so leave me be. Dan 1834.*

NOTES

1. Wikipedia, "Colt Paterson," accessed April 10, 2018, https://en.wikipedia.org/wiki/Colt_Paterson. The firearm industry in America was revolutionized by Samuel Colt's introduction of a gun that could fire five times without reloading. His 1836 version of the Colt pistol was a .28 caliber referred to as the Colt Paterson because it was manufactured in Paterson, New Jersey. The 1839 version of the gun, the Texas Paterson, was a .36 caliber and the famed 1847 Walker Colt was produced as a .44 caliber.

2. Rupert Matthews, *The Illustrated Encyclopedia of Small Arms: From Hand Cannons to Automatic Weapons* (San Diego, CA: Thunder Bay Press, 2014), 130-131. The standard of excellence against which weapons were measured changed with each new revolutionary improvement. Owners of the 1836 to 1838 Colts were grateful for their innovative five-shot capacity and the thought would never have occurred to them to complain they had to almost take the gun apart to insert a new preloaded cylinder. Yet the introduction of the 1839 Colt made all previous versions obsolete. The 1839 Colt was revolutionary in that the near disassembly required with earlier Colts was no longer required and took a fraction of the time to replace with pre-loaded cylinders.

CHAPTER TWO

Gold, a word when whispered or yelled, ignited lust and yearning. I felt my heart pound as though trying to escape from my chest. My eyes quickly swept the area around the old man, half expecting to see a yellow mound sparkling in the dark.

Opening my mouth I drew in as much of the stale cave air as possible and forced myself to breathe. Bending my knees so the torch was closer to the ground, I began to sweep the area. Not five feet away sat ten leather bags as large as canteens, tied and stacked like so much casual baggage.

Fighting back an impulse to rush forward, I slowly walked over, gingerly knelt, and with trembling fingers opened one of the bags. Out poured roughly processed gold with bits of crystal still clinging to the precious metal.

I was not a miner. When camped by a stream I might pan a little, more out of curiosity than anything else. On occasion, my swirling produced gold dust and flakes. I even found a small nugget or two in the Sierras, but never thick veins of gold coursing through quartz. The old man hit the mother lode.

Conscious of the heaviness of the gold in the palm of my hand, I wondered if I was dreaming. Texas possessed no gold mines. The Spanish had an unquenchable thirst for gold. Spaniards found gold everywhere, but rarely in Texas, and never in significant amounts.

With my heart and blood pounding, I went back to the slit of sunlight and restarted my search on a way to escape the cave. Next to the sun beam was a smooth twenty-foot-long wall. The smooth wall met another fifteen-foot wall and at the base of the wall were four roughly constructed ladders. I suspect each time the old miner climbed out of the cave, he knocked down the ladder so no one else would get suspicious and descend into the dark crevice. Upon his return, the miner climbed back down by constructing a new ladder. Since there were four ladders, I assume he made four trips away from the cave.

Four trips sounded about right because against the wall were picks, axes, shovels, buckets, and other mining tools that would require repeated trips to accumulate. The miner had also stored up a collection of canned foods, torches, rags, and oil to keep the torches burning.

Examining the wall the miner was sitting against, it appeared to be close to eighteen feet long. Set into the wall was a small section that looked like it was used for heating the cave and cooking.

The fourth side of the cave was just a long dark tunnel. With my torch held high, I walked into the dark opening and had only traveled thirty feet when it branched. Following the left branch, I went twenty feet and encountered a dead-end.

While retracing my steps, I glanced up and saw a slight overhang. A close examination of the point where the branch started, revealed a small foot and hand hold. Grasping both, I climbed up and noted the overhang trailed back about twenty feet. The recess appeared to be an elevated sleeping area, which was a good idea if there were other rattlesnakes.

Returning to the cave floor I stopped at the right branch and lit a torch anchored head high at the entrance. Thirty feet into the branch I noticed the walls were veined with crystal and gold. The appearance of so much gold in a raw state was mesmerizing. My hand unconsciously went to the wall and came back with lumps of crystal and gold that crumbled between my fingers.

I am not sure what made me stop. Suddenly, I went completely still and listened. My ears caught a faint shushing sound as though the earth was moving, or the floor was shifting. I dropped my torch lower and there not thirty feet away was a swirling nest of rattlers, their angry eyes fixed on me. Seemingly as one, their tails began to rattle, their warning of death echoing off the cave walls.

My entire body shivered with horror. Dreading the answer, I swept the torch outward to see if any snakes blocked my retreat. No snakes were behind me. Shaking, I forced myself to slowly back out of the branch into the main cave. A voice screamed in my head, "Leave. Now!"

Grasping the sturdiest-looking ladder, I stood the wooden contraption up with the top rung leaning against the narrow opening in the ceiling. Testing the bottom rung with my full weight, the ladder held. I grabbed a bag of gold and began climbing up with the hope my horse had not wandered too far in search of food or water.

When my hands cleared the cave opening, I tossed the bag of gold on the ground and re-entered the sunlight. The sudden brightness after the dim cave momentarily blinded me.

Stepping away from the ladder, I heard the click of a gun hammer. Squinting, I slowly turned to see a lump of hair and dirt squatting on a rock ten feet away pointing a flintlock musket at my chest. The deranged-looking hermit holding the .75 caliber Brown Bess began to cackle like a rusty water pump with only a faint memory of water.

"I see you found the mine. For ten long years, I have been looking for that gold. It's a good thing you fell into that hole."

From the madness in the hermit's eyes, it was apparent almost anything I said would be wrong. I wanted to ask him if he shot me, but I knew the answer. I wanted to ask him why he shot me, but I already knew that answer too.

"Slowly reach into your holster and drop that fancy pistol at your feet."

Gingerly I reached down and with my fingertips pulled out the Colt. The Brown Bess had an effective killing range of fifty to one hundred yards. At ten feet, I was as good as dead if I tried anything. With resignation, I gently laid my Colt on the ground.

"Throw me the bag."

Gently I tossed the bag at his feet. With one hand the hermit untied the string and poured a small sample in his wrinkled brown hand. The response was a nerve-racking cackle that scared me. Gold lust weaved with madness was a bad combination.

I only had one chance to get out of this alive. "In the cave are nine more bags. If you let me have one of the bags, I will show you where I hid the gold."

"Sure," he said with a malicious grin that conveyed the opposite intention. I knew he intended to kill me.

"Why don't you go first, and I will follow you down," I agreeably suggested.

I hoped he would find my offer suspicious, and he did. "No sir, you first, and I will follow with my gun. Try anything and I will blow a hole in you. From this distance, it won't be no burn."

Shaking my head as though disappointed, I turned to the ladder. I had gone down five rungs when the hermit's feet hit the first rung above me. With a violent push, I threw myself off the ladder, landed in the debris pile, and rolled into the darkness of the cave.

I sprinted for the cave branches as the old hermit called down, "Don't do you no good to hide, you got no gun."

Ignoring the dim sputtering torch protruding from the branch on the right, I grabbed the unlit torch at the left branch. Quickly locating the hand hold, I climbed up the ledge and laid down flat. The old-timer might not notice the recess, and if he did, he did not have an angle to fire up at me. I could lay next to the edge and if he attempted to climb up, I could use the unlit torch to knock the madman off without being seen.

With no intent to mask his movements, I heard shuffling and the hermit came into the dim light thrown off by the sputtering right branch torch. I saw him grab the torch and wave it in an erratic circle. The old man continued down the right branch. I figure he too got about fifteen feet before he noticed the gold-veined crystal in the wall. A loud maniacal cackle echoed through the cave. After ten years of searching, his gold yearning must have been all-consuming because I heard his feet stomp as he began to run down the branch. His second yell was not of triumph, but of panic.

My senses on high alert, in the suddenly quiet cave I heard a rattler strike at him. In his haste, the hermit twisted and instead of falling toward the branch entrance, he must have fallen back into the nest of rattlers. I heard the sickening thud as numerous rattlers sank their fangs into the stunned man. With amazing speed, the old miner jumped up, ran down the branch, across the cave, and up the ladder.

I stayed where I was. The old miner would not survive for long with that many bites. I slowly began my climb off the ledge checking to see if any rattlers had clung to and dropped off the miner. With a shudder, I was relieved to see no angry snakes barred the way.

Carefully examining the ladder with my torch for rattlesnakes, I grabbed a ladder rung and climbed out of the cave. I looked around for the miner. Surprisingly, he made it thirty feet from the mine entrance before he dropped dead.

CHAPTER THREE

Standing on the rim of the cave, I cupped my hands to my mouth and yelled, "Oh Woe." A hundred yards away Woe was in a three-foot-high stand of sideoats grama, a nutritious grass that blooms in May, and seeds from June to November.[1] Though it was early December, the oat-like seed still clung to the arched grass stems and Woe was getting a well-deserved feeding.

When I called, Woe's head came up and he trotted over, nuzzling me like a big dog. I bought Woe two years ago from a rancher in California. Woe was a bay, sixteen hands high with a beautiful reddish-brown body and a blackish mane, tail, and lower legs.

The widowed rancher shared Woe had been raised by his daughter who was no bigger than the colt when he was born. While watching the colt's birth, the young girl had called out, "Oh woe," her version of, "Oh wow." The name stuck.

My horse was starting to go lame when I stopped at the ranch, and I was reluctantly in the market for a new one. The rancher surprisingly agreed to sell Woe, his best horse. His daughter had been taken by the fever the previous winter, and he could not look at Woe without thinking of the child he lost. I was happy to help the rancher out and he was pleased to see Woe go to a good owner.

Woe and I hit it right off. You would think we could read each other's minds. We knew when the other was tired, hungry, thirsty, or worried.

With Woe resting his head on my shoulder, I sat down right there and considered what to do about the hermit. If I buried him, someone might come looking for him and assume I killed him. Leaving him where he lay, critters might eat him and all evidence of the rattlesnake bites would be gone, leaving someone to assume I killed him. Unfortunately, the best option was to load him up and take him to some town in the vicinity. I needed witnesses that the old hermit died of rattlesnake bites and I had nothing to do with his death.

San Antonio was the closest substantial town.[2] Ninety miles southeast, San Antonio was too big and too far. I needed to take the body to a small town with fewer people to speculate on alternate explanations of his death. Several days prior I had skirted around such a town to the southwest and it would suit my purpose.

Glancing at the sun's position, I knew it was too late to travel and began to set up camp. To Woe's delight, I moved him back to the stand of grama. Walking through the grama, I practically stepped on the old miner's burro laying in the waist-high grass. Braying loudly, the indignant animal lurched up on all fours.

The startled burro looked as wild as the crazy hermit. Burrs, stickers, and bits of grass stuck to its matted grey coat. Only three feet tall, the edge of every rib pressed against its emaciated body. The burro looked to weigh less than one hundred and thirty pounds.

Grabbing the burro's halter, I dragged the skinny beast over to where Woe was eating. I staked out the burro and instead of thanks, the indignant animal brayed a string of burro curses as I departed.

With the animals chomping on the grass, I built a small smokeless fire so that I could cook the rattlesnake that made the mistake of trying to bite me down in the cave. Pulling out my knife, I carefully butchered the snake so that the sixteen rattles stayed connected to the seven-foot skin. I intended to stretch the skin over the fireplace in my next home.

While eating my fill of rattlesnake, the sun sank on the western horizon. Watching a fire burn down has always been calming and helps me think. Staring into the burning embers I decided to return to the cave and bury the gold, take the body into town, and then return for the bags of gold.

I climbed down the ladder and began to search for a good spot to bury the bags of gold. The main cave was stone but had a dirt floor at its lowest point, so I grabbed a shovel and began to dig while keeping an eye out for rattlers. I decided not to kill the rattlers, they would be deadly guardians.

After digging down about twelve inches the shovel made a strange "clunk" sound. Not a "thunk" like when you hit a stone floor. Thrusting the torch down into the hole I saw rows of gold bars. I blinked in shock, not believing my eyes.

Getting down on my hands and knees I began carefully pulling the dirt away. Before I was aware of it, I was clawing at the dirt, throwing dirt in every direction, creating a cloud of dust so thick that it obscured my vision.

I forced myself to stop digging. With great effort, I sat on the edge of the hole and waited for the dust to clear.

With the dust settling, I was able to see that my frantic digging uncovered a pit four feet long and three feet wide. The pit was filled with bars of Spanish gold. Most bars were as long as the distance from the tips of my fingers to the start of my wrist, two fingers wide, and thick as a finger. Some bars, but not many, were double that size.

Trembling, I reached down and picked up first a small bar and then a larger bar. I figured the small bars weighed half a pound and the larger ones a pound. This mine had been lost more than once.

You could tell right off the bars were Spanish from the stamps on them. I had seen similar gold bars in California. When the Spanish first arrived, they molded gold into such bars by filling a rock or wood box with wet sand. They would then jam a rod five inches into the sand to form ingot-sized holes. The gold was melted and poured into the holes. When the gold was cool enough, the ingots were dug up and stamped.

I began to remove the bars to see how deeply they had been stored. After an hour and just two feet into the pit, I stopped. Removing the gold was a waste of effort. I was just going to have to put the bars back in the hole.

Bending down I began to return the gold to the pit. Then I threw the ten bags of quartz gold on top. Carefully I shoveled the dirt back over the treasure and then covered the pit with cave debris. I did not want to leave any evidence of digging.

Discovering the treasure presented me with several problems. How to get the bars out of there without attracting attention? How to get legal possession of the mine?

By the time I climbed out of the cave, the sun's dawn rays were just peeking over the horizon. I was greeted by a cool December morning, but there was no frost on the ground and no need for a coat.

Carefully examining the ground, I erased any trace we had been anywhere near the crevice. Working backward to where the animals grazed, I erased all evidence of our activities leading to the cave.

I laid the miner's body across his protesting burro and headed west toward the town I had skirted around several days ago. Someone in the town might know the miner and come looking for him. Better that I turn his body over at the town and explain that I found the old guy covered in rattlesnake bites.

• • •

Three mornings later, I rode into a mere shadow of a town. One glance revealed a saloon, an abandoned general store, and several sun-bleached shacks where people must live. Being so small, any event was a big affair, so when a rider shows up with a body, everyone came out into the dusty street to see what was happening.

I looked around the curious faces and said, "Howdy, coming up the trail I noticed a burro without a rider and then found the rider. Looks like this old timer got bit by a nest of rattlers. Anyone here kin to him?"

"That is old Moss," said a stooped grey-haired man.

After three days the body was bloated and smelled a touch poorly. The smell could have been worse. Texas was experiencing a December that was not hot enough to raise a sweat nor cold enough to freeze water. Thanks to the cool weather the old miner's body was only a little rank.

"That was a hard man," commented someone.

"Yep, it's been said he went mad and starting shooting at people in the desert."

"Looks like his luck finally ran out," remarked one gnarly old man with a tobacco juice-stained beard.

Everyone just awkwardly stood around staring at the body, every piece of exposed skin showing inflamed fang marks.

"You got a graveyard?" I asked.

"Not much to speak of, got two or three bodies and some body parts down by that old mesquite tree."

"Do you have someone to bury him, or do I have to?" I asked a little irritably.

"Jim, go get some shovels, we got nothing else to do," suggested the least decrepit member of the group. With that command, the crowd of five began moving toward the tree and someone grabbed the little burro's reins.

"You got any feed for my horse?"

"Sorry stranger, nothing for your horse. Likewise, if you are thirsty we got nothing but homemade rotgut we only drink out of desperation ourselves. Since the mercantile failed, we haven't had much of anything around here. Too many Comanche attacks, they come right up into town."

I was delighted to hear there was no reason to remain. Sighing, I shook my head as though sad to hear it. "Well, I have done my civic duty. I did not want that old-timer to rot away in the desert or get carried off by critters. With nothing for me or my horse, I will be on my way. How far to the next town?"

NOTES

1. Brian Loflin and Shirley Loflin, *Grasses of the Texas Hill Country* (College Station, TX: Texas A&M University Press, 2006), 47.

2. The gold mine would be located in what is today called the Lost Maples Texas State Natural Area. The area was unsettled by Anglos until the 1850s (and periodically abandoned) because it was first an Apache stronghold and then part of the Comanche Trace (pathway from the north to raid in the south). Today Lost Maples lays five miles north of Vanderpool, fifteen miles north of Utopia, ninety miles northwest of San Antonio, and 157 miles southwest of Austin.

CHAPTER FOUR

Rather than returning to the mine, I headed to Austin which was a seven to eight-day ride northeast. Though no one seemed interested in me, it was prudent not to lead anyone back to the gold.

Each night on the trail I thought about the things I needed to do. First, I had to file a claim to the land over the mine. Second, getting word to my kin to join me was critical. Third, I needed to build a defensible dwelling over the mine entrance in case someone tried to take it away. Fourth, the gold belonged in a bank.

On my last night on the trip, I camped five miles from Austin. Sprawled out on a blanket staring at the stars, I recited my plan. When word of the gold got out, every thief and politician within five hundred miles would be out to skin me and take the mine.

To get the land, I would have to trade something very precious to me, papers from the Republic of Texas entitling me to claim land. The head of all households present in Texas before March 4, 1836, were eligible for First Class Headright land grants of 4,605 acres, while single men received 1,476 acres.[1] All volunteers who served honorably in the Army of the Republic of Texas, were entitled to a Bounty grant of 320 acres for every three months served with a maximum total of 1,280 acres.[2] If a man died defending Texas, his heirs received a Bounty grant of 640 acres.[3] There were also Donation grants of 640 acres for fighting in specific battles such as San Jacinto, Bexar, Harrisburg, and others.[4]

I had a 1,280-acre Bounty grant for serving, 1,280 acres in Donation grants for two specific battles, the 640-acre Bounty grant because my father died during the war, and my 1,476 First Class Headright acres for a total of 4,676. I kept the land certificates in a secret compartment in my saddlebags for the past three years. Having my papers close was a comfort.

After the war, some folks sold their vouchers to profiteers who offered hard cash, but little of it. Being offered five percent of its value was criminal. Unfortunately, many people had no choice. Folks were so poor after the Texas Revolution with their stock stolen and crops burned that they were glad to get anything.

I lay there in the dark trying to recall the last time I traveled to the area now called Austin,[5] the new capital of the Republic of Texas. When I left Texas in late 1836 there was a great deal of arguing about the location of the new Republic's capital. After the Convention of 1836, there were temporary capitals at Washington-on-the-Brazos, Harrisburg, Galveston, and Velasco, with then supposedly permanent capitals at Columbia and Houston before they finally settled on Austin three months ago.[6]

My reverie was interrupted when Woe's head snapped up. I had camped alone many a time and was nobody's fool. During my travels west and back, I had developed the habit of stashing grass or a small bush next to my bedroll. With a simple flip, the bedroll would cover the bush as though it was me, while I crawled quietly to a defensive spot I always built in my camps. In this case, it was a log conveniently dragged just outside the light of my small campfire.

Quickly I scampered away and lay down with my head and body hidden behind the length of the log. I patiently lay there, my pistol in hand.

Though I was alert, I was jolted by the three rifle shots that hammered into my now-empty bed. With the shots still echoing in the night, I heard the empty rifles thrown to the ground as new guns were picked up and cocked. Into the dim firelight walked three hard men, confident they had committed murder.

Using the toe of his boot, one outlaw threw back the pock-marked blanket with his toe. I popped my pistol onto the log and commanded, "Drop your guns."

Since the log was outside the dim firelight, they assumed I was standing and fired chest-high in my direction. From my prone position, I fired my Colt in rapid succession. Twenty feet away my first slug hit the shortest of the three, right above the nose, blowing his brains all over the other two. A tall-bearded man next to him took a bullet in the chest and one in the arm as he twisted away. The last hard case caught two in the belly.

To say I shot them to rags from that distance would be accurate. I did not shoot to wound. These men tried to kill me and needed to die trying.

Back east people said it was wrong to kill. They contended you should warn people sufficiently to convince them to stop. If warnings did not work, they argued you should shoot them in the hand or leg.

People who said such foolish things have never faced a killer. If they had, those gentle souls would not be talking now, they would be singing in the afterlife. My goal was to delay joining the choir.

I quickly popped out the Colt's spent cylinder and inserted a preloaded cylinder. Carrying two extra preloaded cylinders was a precaution for me. Switching cylinders was faster than laboriously tapping in five new paper cartridges.

After reloading the gun, I stayed on the ground waiting for the smoke to clear. When five minutes passed, I crawled around to the other side of camp and came in from the opposite direction from where I shot. I studied the situation and detected no movement. Walking in, I threw another log on the fire to light up the scene.

When I rolled the killers over, their dead eyes revealed their souls had been dragged to hell, leaving behind their bloody bodies. The killers were fairly shot to hell. At point-blank range, my .36 caliber slugs drilled clean holes going in, and as the lead flattened, blew large holes coming out.

The prospect of sleeping with three dead bodies was unattractive, so I threw more wood on the fire lighting up the campsite as bright as day. While rolling up my bedroll, I counted three bullet holes. Well, they paid dearly for those holes. I gathered up my cooking utensils, packed my gear, and while saddling Woe, thanked him for the warning.

A short search revealed the killers had tied their horses to brush fifty yards from camp. I gathered the reins of one horse and led her back to camp. The mare was a beautiful blond chestnut with a light tan coat and even lighter mane and tail.

Tying the reins to the log, I threw the outlaw's body across the saddle. The horse may or may not have liked the outlaws alive, but she certainly did not like them dead. Nostrils flaring, the unhappy mare danced sideways, and the body slid off the saddle agitating the horse even more.

Rather than push the issue, I patted the mare's neck and gave her some time to calm down.

I retrieved the second horse, a crème-colored bay with a blackish mane, tail, and legs. Such a horse is commonly called a buckskin, but some argue they are bays. The horse did not like the smell of blood in the camp. He pranced in protest as I threw the body across the saddle but settled down as I stroked his neck. I tied the body securely and it did not slide off.

The third horse, a magnificent bay seventeen hands high, acted like this was not the first time he carried a body. The bay was dark, almost as dark as the seals I had seen in California. His mane, tail, and legs were jet black. I looked him in the eye and said, "I wonder who owned you? You are too good a horse for the likes of these hombres."

By the time I finished with the other two horses, the skittish mare had calmed down. Speaking softly, I let her know it was a short ride into Austin. The chestnut mare let me tie the outlaw across her back but turned her head to eye the lifeless body.

Walking down to the creek I hauled enough water to turn the fire into a mudhole. I was never one to chance setting a forest or prairie on fire.

After double-checking each of the bodies, I tied the outlaws' guns down securely behind their saddles. Each had a rifle and a musket, two of them had a brace of pistols.

Tying the reins of the three horses to the horse in front of it, I began the wearisome task of riding while trailing three disgruntled horses behind me. The first mile, Woe kept turning his head to look at me and rolling his eyes in disgust. I was a sore disappointment to Woe at times.

• • •

When I arrived at the outskirts of Austin, I inquired about the whereabouts of the Texas Rangers Headquarters. Though not an official organization at the beginning, Stephen F. Austin planted the seeds for the Texas Rangers in 1823 when he hired ten men to protect the new settlers he brought to Texas.[7] In 1835, the Texas Rangers were officially established, and at any one time, there were between three and six companies of Rangers paid one dollar and twenty-five cents a day to protect the Republic.[8]

The Republic of Texas was enormous, stretching over a thousand miles east to west and north to south.[9] Due to the distance they had to cover, Rangers went out alone or in small groups. Such men were self-sufficient and hard. You did not want to get on the wrong side of the Rangers.

While tying Woe and the other three horses in front of the Ranger Headquarters, a crowd began to gather. People starting shouting questions about the bodies, pestering me like swirling gnats. I ignored their questions.

I walked into the building and with a voice that sounded more confident than I felt, asked, "Can you tell me who is in charge?"

A bowl-legged man who looked like dried-up leather stepped forward. "How can I help you?"

"Five miles out of town three fellers shot my bedroll to pieces. I did not approve of them treating my property that way, especially since they thought I was in the bedroll. When I told them to drop their guns they shot at me. I returned the favor. Their bodies are tied to their horses."

My story was met by silence. Though the Ranger's face did not move, I got the uncomfortable feeling he was sizing me up. After a full three minutes of staring, the Ranger picked up a stack of handbills decorated with outlaws' faces and descriptions.

"Let's see the deceased," he said.

I followed him out the door. He lifted the first man's head and studied it intently from every direction. The stern Ranger pulled out a handbill and said, "Here, hold this."

He repeated the process two more times. Without saying another word, the bowl-legged old-timer wobbled back into the building with authority. I stood there flatfooted and then decided I should probably follow him.

Once inside he perched on the edge of a desk and said, "Start from the beginning."

A little exasperated, I started from the beginning with Woe's warning and ended with the ride into town. When I finished he said, "I am Captain Jim Eldridge, would you like a job with the Rangers?"

I was too stunned to respond. It was my turn to stare at him. Finally, I said, "Captain Eldridge, sir. I served in the Texas Revolution and have traveled to the Mexican territories in California and back several times.

This is not the first time I have killed men. I hope those three men outside are the last. I want no more killing."

Captain Eldridge shook his head, "Understood."

"You performed Texas a favor. Those outlaws killed innocent men and even women. We have been hunting them. You did us all a service."

"Each of those men is a killer and has a reward on their head. Let us see, one hundred, seventy-five, and one hundred dollars. The total is two hundred and seventy-five dollars. I will write you an official Republic of Texas voucher that any bank will cash. What was your name?"

"Forgive my lack of manners Captain Eldridge. My name is Rye, Rye Campise."

Pointing outside to where the horses stood tied to the railings, I said, "Thank you, Captain Eldridge. Collecting money for killing those men is not something I can do. I bet you have some kind of fund for Ranger widows and orphans. Please give the money to them."

The Ranger nodded, "Mighty kind of you. In addition, you are also entitled to their horses and gear, provided they are not stolen."

Deliberating for a moment, I said, "They had some mighty fine horses. I would be happy to take the horses and their weapons. You can never have too many guns."

Hesitantly I said, "One of the outlaws had a book, I like to read. I would be appreciative if I could have the book."

Captain Eldridge nodded, "Sure. If you like books the mercantile has several for sale or trade."

"I was headed there just now. Can I come back in several hours for the horses and guns?"

Captain Eldridge shook his head and said, "I will copy the brands on those horses and let you know if anyone shows up to claim ownership. In the meantime, I will see that your horse and the other three are fed and watered."

Exiting the building, the crowd parted to let me through. So much for keeping a low profile.

NOTES

1. Texas General Land Office, "Categories of Land Grants," accessed April 5, 2018, www.glo.texas.gov/history/archives/forms/files/glo-headright-military-land-grants.pdf.
2. Ibid.
3. Ibid.
4. Ibid.
5. John Holmes Jenkins III, ed., Recollections of Early Texas (Austin, TX: University of Texas Press, 1958, 1975), 252. Footnote refers to the fourth reprint in 1975. Mr. and Mrs. Anderson Harrell built the first house where Austin now stands. When the Harrell's built their home, the town was called Waterloo, and later became known as Austin.
6. Handbook of Texas Online, John G. Johnson, "Capitals," accessed May 10, 2018, https://www.tshaonline.org/handbook/online/articles/mzc01. The capital site selection committee bought 7,735 acres along the Colorado River, including the hamlet of Waterloo.
7. Wikipedia, "Texas Ranger Division," accessed May 4, 2018, https://en.wikipedia.org/wiki/Texas_Ranger_Division.
8. Texas Department of Public Safety, "Texas Rangers Historical Development," accessed April 28, 2020, http://www.dps.texas.gov/TexasRangers/HistoricalDevelopment.thml. Each company of Rangers consisted of fifty-six men led by a Captain, First Lieutenants, and Second Lieutenants. A Major provided overall command of the Rangers.
9. Wikipedia, "Republic of Texas," accessed April 24, 2021, https://en.wikipedia.org/wiki/Republic_of_Texas. The state of Texas is appropriately viewed as enormous. Many however are unaware the original boundaries of the Republic of Texas were substantially larger. The original boundaries included not only the current state of Texas, but also parts of what would become the states of New Mexico, Colorado, Wyoming, Oklahoma, and Kansas.

CHAPTER FIVE

The first person I encountered pointed out the land office, a two-story wooden building still under construction. Once I knew what to look for, there was no missing the big Texas General Land Office sign designed to project an air of prosperity for the new Republic.

Opening the door, I walked into a huge room that filled the entire bottom floor of the unfinished building. The walls were lined with books and maps in English, Spanish, and even French. Hunched over an expansive ten-foot-by-five-foot oak table, a neatly combed bearded gentleman in a vest with an excess of pockets was gently flipping enormous maps. I hesitated to interrupt, so I quietly walked over to the table and waited.

"Ah, there lies the error," he said with satisfaction to himself. Looking up with a welcoming smile he declared, "Texas is fortunate Spain diligently mapped every foot of land it crossed. The Spaniards believed by being the first to document the land they were entitled to claim it. French maps are also detailed, but primarily in laying out the waterways for commerce. Fortunately, early Texans documented their travels and the landscape, not for ownership purposes, but to understand the land they encountered."

Grateful at the opportunity to expand my understanding of early Texas, I said, "Please continue, I did not mean to interrupt."

A smile of apology flashed across the land manager's face and was quickly replaced with delight at the chance to discuss one of his favorite topics, maps. "I did not mean to ignore you, but I was reconciling a discrepancy on three maps. I suspect the maps differ because the Spanish map is one hundred and fifty years old while the Texas map is only three years old. Rivers change course over time as rivers are want to do, and I suspect that is why they differ."

Putting the maps aside, he said, "What can I do for you?"

"My name is Rye Campise, and I found some water south and west of town and wanted to file a claim to it."

Performing a mock bow, he stuck out his hand and said, "Robert Eldridge, nice to meet you. My friends call me Zeke."

The land agent pulled out a large Republic of Texas map and several smaller maps of my area of interest. He said, "One of the best ways of agreeing on a location is by following the waterways. The Frio River starts twenty or so miles northwest of you and runs south ten miles from your place. Five or so miles north of you the Medina River starts and runs east for forty miles before turning south. The Sabinal River is a simple spring several miles north of there, becomes a threadbare creek through the land you have chosen, increases in volume to a stream, and transitions into a river south of you."

Nodding agreement, I said, "The streams run wet and dry before they have a constant flow. In addition to the stream bed, I found seeps and several artesian wells. When I moved some rocks, the hole filled with clear drinkable water. I suspect I can enlarge the hole and it will provide enough water for me while I do some mining and run some cows."

"You can try. If memory serves me correct, that land is more canyon wall than pasture. Meadows can be found on top of the canyons and further south. Most of that land consists of jagged two thousand-foot mountains with three canyons that meander through them. Your canyon contains the headwaters of the Sabinal River. The canyon to the left has Can Creek running through its bottom. To the far left is a canyon that possesses a trickle of water so insubstantial it has no name. South of those canyon mouths lay some nice stretches of meadow with the canyon walls spreading out to form a pleasant valley."

"Thanks for the recommendation, but for now I prefer a wild place nobody else will want."

With a nod, he said, "Well, best of luck to you. Stake the four corners of the land you are claiming and stake what you claim as your homestead acres separately. The new Texas laws were written to protect people from getting kicked out of their homes. A single adult can claim one hundred acres as his homestead, and the head of a family can claim two hundred."[1]

Pointing to the map, I said, "This spot right here will be my homestead."

Nodding, he said, "Did you want to purchase any additional land?"

Reluctantly, I handed over my land vouchers. Looking over the crumpled papers, he asked, "Did you buy them or earn them?"

Much rougher than intended, I said, "I earned all of those damned papers."

With a gentle voice, he replied, "My apologies, after the war a lot of good people sold their land drafts for five cents to the dollar. I congratulate you on surviving and keeping your land vouchers."

He held up one of the papers and said, "My condolences, if you have this paper your father died in the war."

I replied, "Yep." Neither of us said anything for several minutes. We just stood there, not awkwardly, just in silent understanding.

Laying the certificates down one at a time, Zeke counted out, "First Class Headright land grant for 1,476 acres, a Bounty land grant for 1,280 acres, a Bounty land grant for 640 acres, and two Donation grants at 640 acres each. Your land grants total 4,676 acres."

Nodding in agreement, I said, "I want to buy some additional acreage to round that up to five thousand." With a grimace, I handed over a small pile of paper money and metal coins. I was gold-rich, but cash-poor. The gold could not be used until my family arrived and helped me secure the land.

With the hundred-acre homestead as a starting point, I began to select the land I wanted. After helping me identify my boundaries, Zeke pulled out multiple pieces of paper and began to draw three amazingly accurate maps.

"These maps serve as legal documents. I will need to put down your given name as the holder of the land." With a smile, Zeke said, "I don't mean to insult you. But I doubt your parents named you after a type of whiskey or a variety of grass. Is Rye your legal name?"

Shaking my head, I hesitantly said, "No, but it's a long story."

To this, the land manager pulled up a chair and sat down. With a sigh, I said, "In 1808 Henry Lee III was recommissioned as a major-general by

President Thomas Jefferson because it looked like the United States of America might be going to war with Great Britain. While riding through the countryside organizing the Virginia militia, General Lee stopped by the farm where my mother was being raised. She brought a mug of clear spring water to the fence and implored the general to pause for a drink."

"The general, decked out in his tailored uniform with shiny medals galore pinned every which way, stepped off his stallion, and bowed grandly before my mother. General Lee kissed my mother's hand and declared she was the most beautiful thing he had ever seen. Well, you can imagine the impact that had on a ten-year-old country girl."

"Following that visit, my mother read everything she could about 'Light-Horse Harry.' She learned he was the ninth governor of Virginia, a delegate to the Continental Congress, and a cavalry hero of the Revolutionary War.[2] She declared the middle name of any child she bore would be Lee."

"When my dear mother birthed me, I was christened Ricky Lee Campise. That name served me well for nine years. On my tenth birthday, I declared to my parents I was now a man and Ricky Lee was a child's name. I insisted everyone call me Riley, a combination of Ricky and Lee."

"Things sort of backfired, and people just called me Rye. Over time I stopped fighting the name. Now I answer to Rye. Back to your question, I guess your paper should have my given name, Ricky Lee. You might want to add Rye to that just so there is no confusion."

Writing my name as directed, Zeke said, "I drew three maps. One for you, one for the General Land Office, and one for the Republic Archives, which is what we call the Records Office. After you stake out your claim, return so that we can amend the maps to ensure they are as accurate as possible."

"Will do."

I headed toward the door as the land manager called after me, "In case you do not know, the area you are settling in is called Lost Maples. Unlike any other area in Texas, there are two canyons full of bigtooth maple trees and you appear to have purchased land in one of the canyons. Ten or eleven months from now the two canyon bottoms light up in an explosion of red, orange, yellow, amber, and gold."

Halting at the door, I tilted my head to the side and said, "You appear pretty knowledgeable about a wide part of Texas."

"Young man, I was a botany professor at an eastern university a lifetime ago. I count myself lucky to have been a member of the Old Three Hundred and to have received a land grant in Stephen F. Austin's first colony in 1824.[3] Heck, I even came to Texas with Stephen in 1821 before the Old Three Hundred. From my first visit, I fell in love with this wild land. I have spent more of the past eighteen years wandering around Texas than I care to tell."

Out of respect, I nodded and asked, "Should I call you Dr. or Professor Eldridge?"

"No, no, please call me Zeke." Hesitantly he reached under the counter and pulled out a book he handed to me with an embarrassed smile. "Every couple of years I publish a book that includes trees, bushes, and flowers I have encountered in Texas. The books are not for sale. I give them to people on the condition they share with me any new information I can add to the next edition. Would you like one?"

Smiling broadly, I said, "Absolutely. I have a small library of a dozen books, but I will not put your book on the shelf with them. While riding I will carry your book with me and try to add information about Lost Maples."

"Excellent," the delighted professor replied. "There is no section on mammals of Texas, but I hope to add it one of these days. The Indians claim animals have moved north over time from Mexico to areas like Lost Maples. Those include the javelina, bears, and black cougars the Mexicans call panthers."

I smiled at the book in my hand and said, "I will take note of what I see and leave it to you to shift through it for anything useful." A sudden thought hit me, and I said, "Are you any relation to Captain Eldridge of the Rangers?"

Zeke nodded, "Before meeting Captain Eldridge we did not know we were related. Conversing with him over whiskey late one night, we discovered we shared a common ancestor. We both descended from the same Eldridge who was ordered out of England one hundred and twenty years ago on a charge of sedition. After several generations, most of the

Eldridge descendants ended up in Virginia, but others spread out to other states. Now several of us unknown relations find ourselves in Texas."

Standing to leave, I said, "I suspect my brother Darryl and several others will be joining me soon. Would you mind helping them pick land next to mine?"

Walking out the door I was filled with newfound wonder. You just never know who is going to show up in Texas. I sure missed this country. Since leaving Texas I had spent my time exploring the great expanse between the coast of California and the border of the new Republic. In my heart, there was always an ache to return to Texas.

During the Texas Revolution, I killed people and watched people I cared about die. The last straw was when my father caught a ball standing next to me and just died in my arms. I felt like a hot brand seared something deep inside of me. I was not sad, just unsettled and nothing seemed to settle me down.

Following their defeat at the Battle of San Jacinto in 1836, the Mexican Army agreed to leave Texas. Since I was a member of the Army of the People and not serving an enlistment with the Army of the Republic of Texas, I just had to notify one of the officers we elected and tell him I needed some open space and wanted to be alone. [4] I wandered for three and a half years. Wandering helped a little, but not a lot.

Spying a sign for the post office, I walked down and wrote a letter to my brother Darryl. The letter was short, "Homesteading. You, Dennis, and Kel claim land near my homestead at Lost Maples 7.14.12.4."

The numbers at the end were a code that Darryl and I used growing up. We numbered the alphabet and tested each other by saying numbers instead of words. Our code was a convenient way to determine who got the last piece of the pie.

Darryl would know the numbers spelled "gold" and would stop whatever he was doing. I planned to return to the mine and build a stone house on top of the mine entrance that could withstand any attack.

NOTES

1. FindLaw, "Texas Homestead Law Overview," accessed May 3, 2018, https://statelaws.findlaw.com/texas-law/texas-homestead-law-overview.html. The numbers provided apply to rural homesteads. An urban homestead is limited to ten acres.

2. Wikipedia, "Henry Lee III," accessed June 7, 2018, https://en.wikipedia.org/wiki/Henry_Lee_III.

3. Wikipedia, "Old Three Hundred," accessed April 16, 2018, https://en.wikipedia.org/wiki/Old_Three_Hundred. This reference names each of the Old Three Hundred (actually 297). The list includes their names, dates of birth and death, and family members as of March 26, 1826. Also included are notes of worth regarding the list, such as identifying Thomas McKinney as the Father of the Texas Navy, and Zaddock Woods as the oldest man killed in the Dawson Expedition.

4. *Handbook of Texas Online*, Paul D. Lack, "Revolutionary Army," accessed March 11, 2020, https://tshaonline.org/handbook/online/articles/qjr03. The armed forces that defeated Santa Anna consisted of a confusing mix of groups representing Texas. There was the officially sanctioned Army of the Republic of Texas commanded by Sam Houston. But there was also a group of "independent volunteers," true citizen-soldiers who turned out in a crisis and then returned home to their farms. These volunteers refused the Army's concept of enlistment for a set period and chaffed at the Army's stern discipline which they perceived as constraining their liberties. These men formed themselves into units (often geographically based), democratically elected their leaders/officers, and often participated in tactical decisions. The volunteers infuriated the politicians and the regular army. Yep, as a native Texan, I can accurately say Texans have been hard-headed since the beginning.

CHAPTER SIX

Seeking to avoid trouble, I bypassed the saloons and instead went down to the mercantile. Something quickens your blood when you walk into a well-stocked store and see all the goods stacked floor to ceiling.

I intended to pick up some of the items already in the cave such as picks and shovels. People might rightly wonder if I claimed to mine gold but had never purchased any mining equipment.

My mouth watered as I picked up coffee beans, bacon, flour, and a variety of other perishable items absent from the cave. Thumbing through all the store's treasures, I came across something that set my mind racing. On the counter, stacked three high were molds for making lead balls and bullets. Next to the molds were several cast iron pots for melting lead. Every time I picked up one of the pots I spied another pot even bigger. Staring at the pots, I heard a swishing sound as someone came up behind me.

A female voice said, "I see you admiring those cast iron pots."

Swiveling my head to glance over my shoulder, not a foot away stood a young woman with freckles all over her nose and chin framed by golden-red hair. I stared for what must have been minutes. She arched her right eyebrow at me as though silently asking whether I possessed the capacity of speech.

With a laugh, I said, "Oh I do, but I only have a horse. I don't think he would appreciate the weight, even if I could tie them on."

A beautiful smile lit up her face, setting her freckles to dancing. "I would be interested in seeing that myself." Placing her hands on her hips, she declared, "We do sell wagons."

"I don't need a wagon."

"My dad has something that might interest you. His contraption is a cross between a wagon and a cart. I call it the 'wart,' but he does not like that name."

She continued, "The wart has an oak axle and metal-rimmed oak wheels. Bamboo from down on the river bottoms is used for the frame. The wagon looks a little strange, but it is amazingly light, and a single horse can pull it without strain."

Jutting her head, she indicated I was to follow. I must admit my eyes strayed to her backside. Realizing how embarrassing it would be if she caught me staring so boldly I shifted my eyes to the floor. Unfortunately, I would find my eyes drifting to her backside and again immediately shift my focus to the floor. During one of the backside floor staring episodes, I was not paying attention and when she stopped, I bumped into her. To keep from knocking her over, I grabbed her by the hips. Blood rushed to my beet-red face as I recoiled backward anticipating an indignant slap to my face.

To my amazement, she displayed a hint of a smile and said, "If you would keep your eyes off my backside you would not need to stare at the floor."

Every bit of blood reversed course and rushed out of my face. With a mixture of severity and levity, she said, "You look a bit faint. Why don't you sit on that hay bale while I point out the wart's features?"

She went on to talk about the wheels, the axle, the leather reins, etc. Only I did not hear a single word she said. Instead, I was in a silent world of shame and embarrassment. I just sat there nodding my head. By the time she finished, I had purchased their sturdiest wagon pulled by a team of mules.

I was awash with regret as every penny I owned lay on the counter. By the time the cost of the goods, pots, team, and wagon was added, I had spent all my money and was noticeably short. I stood frozen, unsure what to do. Since the moment I entered the door I had weaved from one embarrassment to another.

"Would your father, I mean you, be interested in trading for some guns to reduce the total?"

"Depends on the guns," she responded.

"I will be back shortly." With that, I trotted back to the Rangers and loaded up half the guns.

When I returned with an arm full of guns she raised her eyebrows, "Do you always carry so many guns?"

"No, they were a recent inheritance."

She picked up one of the three British-made Brown Bess' and said, "These Land Pattern muskets are pretty common. They were the standard weapon of the Mexican infantry, so we Texans captured quite a few during the war. Sure, these front muzzle loaders can load three rounds every minute, but they are only effective at fifty to one hundred yards."[1]

"This musket has not been kept clean and the barrel has been fouled too many times. I doubt even if the barrel is bored out that a .75 caliber ball can be safely fired. You are lucky this musket is so common, I can use it for parts."

Fingering the flintlock on the second Brown Bess she said, "This will have to be replaced." The stock on the third Brown Bess was cracked and she gave out a deep sigh.

With embarrassment, I placed a brace of Harper Ferry Model 1805 single-shot smoothbore flintlock pistols on the counter. Frowning, she lifted them up and with a bit of sarcasm said, "Look at these beauties, only thirty-five years old. I don't have any .54 caliber slugs, but I guess we can have some made up."

Embarrassed as I was, I was no fool. I needed to keep the best outlaw weapons, three rifles and a brace of pistols, for my protection. One was a Kentucky long rifle whose spiral barrel lent stability to the .48 caliber slug. The gun was seventy inches long with a forty-eight-inch barrel and a beautiful birds-eye maple stock. Though I had not fired this rifle, I knew in a skilled man's hands, it had an effective firing range of two hundred yards and could be fired twice a minute.[2]

From the dead outlaws, I also inherited two British Baker rifles that at some point probably belonged to officers in the Mexican Army. The Pattern 1803 was a single shot with a thirty-three-inch barrel used by sharpshooters that could be fired accurately twice per minute at targets two hundred yards away, with some hits two and even three times that distance.[3] Though originally a flintlock, it had been converted to a percussion cap. Since it was still a .62 caliber I knew it had not been overused. With too much use, the barrels had to be bored to a larger caliber, often to a .75 caliber.

The second Baker rifle had a shorter barrel at thirty inches and was probably used by a Mexican Army cavalry officer. Not only was the brass engraved, but it also was inlaid with carved sliver bits.

With the brace of pistols and three decrepit Brown Bess' leaving me far short I asked, "Would you be interested in a couple of saddles and a horse?"

Turning her head to the side she questioned, "Are they also recent inheritances?"

Quickly returning to the Ranger Headquarters, with embarrassment I explained to Captain Eldridge my need to trade one of the horses and two of the saddles. With a trace of a smile, he told me where to get the buckskin and the saddles.

On the return trip to the mercantile, I carried one saddle over my shoulder while leading the saddled buckskin. We engaged in good-natured but fair dickering over each item. Even after all the guns, saddles, and the buckskin, I was still thirty dollars short. Warm fingers tapped my wrist and I looked up into gentle eyes surrounded by glowing freckles. "By opening a store account, you will have to return to see me and pay the balance."

I practically floated out that door and into my new wagon. Driving my new team to the Ranger Headquarters, the cast iron pots rattled and clanged with every bump. I could not decide if I was the biggest sucker in the world or the luckiest man alive.

Walking into the building a dozen Rangers greeted me like we were long-lost brothers. They thanked me for taking out the three outlaws and contributing the rewards to the Ranger's fund. My new-found Ranger friends pitched in to load up the few remaining guns I inherited from the outlaws and helped tie the horses to the back of the wagon.

Riding out of town, I counted myself fortunate to be on the right side of the Rangers. They were a salty crew. I was feeling downright lucky. I survived a killing, inherited two fine horses, three rifles, and two pistols. Best of all, there was a red-headed gal in Austin I sure was excited about visiting again.

NOTES

1. Wikipedia, "Brown Bess," accessed February 10, 2018, https://en.wikipedia.org/wiki/Brown_Bess.

2. Lonn Taylor, "Remember the Long Rifle," *Texas Monthly* (March 2015), https://www.texasmonthly.com/the-culture/remember-the-long-rifle/.

3. Military Factory, "Baker Rifle," accessed April 8, 2018, https://www.militaryfactory.com/smallarms/detail.asp?smallarms_id=925.

CHAPTER SEVEN

Before the trip, I anticipated covering the one hundred and fifty miles back to Lost Maples in six days on horseback. Driving a wagon, I would be lucky to make it in twelve to fourteen days.

My journey was further complicated by the fact I now had three horses to care for on the return. The two outlaw horses were tied to the back of the wagon and were not happy with the arrangement. Woe was allowed him to roam free, when called, Woe would always return.

On the way to Lost Maples, I thought about how I might improve the wagon to haul gold to Austin. The wheels, axles, and frame were all sturdy and in no need of improvement. Copying the mercantile idea of using bamboo to lighten the wagon seemed like a good idea. In my mind, I began to remove the heavy oak boards from the sides and bench. The lighter the wagon, the more gold I could carry to Austin.

Around noon on the second day, I saw the tracks of unshod ponies. I could tell they were not wild horses, they followed each other in single file. My jaw tightened and without thinking about it, my right hand dropped to the pistol on my hip.

Each day my anxiety grew, hovering like some beast on the horizon, impatiently straining for the opportunity to devour me. My eyes and ears were wide open to danger. Ready for a twist in the trail, a dangerous slope, Indians, outlaws, or even someone down on their luck ready to take advantage of an unsuspecting traveler. Failure to pay attention meant death.

Danger occupied my thoughts during the day, but not at night. When I lay down the girl with red hair and freckles occupied my thoughts. I repeated every word she said, the movement of her hands, the edges of her smile, the crinkle around her eyes, and other things better not to mention. The worst of it was, I did not even know her name.

A part of me thought I was a fool for buying the wagon. Yep, a foolish man snookered by a girl. Another part of me knew she was not the kind of girl to take advantage of a man. The truth is she convinced me to buy what I should have looked to buy in the first place. Buying the best wagon was smart. The wagon enabled me to haul those cast iron pots and the mining gear back to camp. Those pots were essential for melting the gold. More importantly, this wagon was stout enough to haul gold to Austin.

On the sixth day out of Austin, I awoke to a crisp December morning. The weather was not cold enough to freeze water, but the nip in the air made my boiling hot cup of coffee that much more enjoyable to drink.

I was a man who followed the calendar closely. By my recollection, today was Christmas, my fourth Christmas alone. With any luck, this was my last Christmas without family.

Arriving back at the mine mid-day on day twelve of the return portion of the trip, I put all thoughts of red hair and freckles from my mind. By my calculations, today was the first day of 1840, a new start, and my birthday.

When I was a young man, my mother told me I refused to be born at the end of an old year struggling on its last legs. I insisted on waiting until the first day of a brand-new year to enter the world. According to my mother, since birth, I was always looking for some new experience over the horizon.

After unloading the wagon, I immediately began the task of staking out my one hundred homestead acres. Smiling with the pride of ownership, I studied the landscape closely. I needed sufficient room in case the gold branch changed course on me. The sad truth was people could, and did, take your land for all kinds of crooked reasons. Thankfully in the Republic of Texas, the land you claimed as your homestead was considered sacred. No court would let someone take it lightly.

With great care, I laid out the hundred homestead acres to include all possible branches of the gold mine, the artesian well, and the meadow already enjoyed by Woe. I drove stakes in the ground and laid out stone corners five rocks high to mark my boundary. With my arms spread wide and feeling a bit full of myself, I proclaimed it, "Lost Maples Ranch."

The first night I built the fire away from the mine entrance and pretended to sleep. In the middle of the night when the fire burned down, I tied a rope off and carefully dropped into the cave with an eye out for rattlesnakes. Over several trips, I hauled up several axes, a file to keep the axes sharp, and canned goods to supplement the game I shot.

Long before the dawn's first rays, I awoke with a grand feeling. I was a property owner and rich to boot.

Grabbing an ax, I walked the canyon getting a feel for the type of trees in my new home. I was delighted to come across spindly tree trunks I recognized as peach, plum, and cherry trees that would produce fruit in late summer. In the bottom of the canyon where there was water, grew cypress, willow, immense pecan, and towering cottonwood trees. Every type of oak populated the mountain tops, hanging steadfastly to the canyon walls, and spreading out across the valley. Alone or in clumps, grew mesquite, juniper, and cedar. Sprinkled across the landscape were madrone, creosote, and agarita bushes.

Great thought went into selecting trees that would be easy to haul to the home site for lumber. Cutting down a tree that required days to drag to the house would be a poor use of my time and end up with the log splintered in the dragging.

Once the right trees were cut, the mule team easily dragged the carefully chosen logs to the house site. With a sharp ax, I trimmed the trees, keeping the trunks and larger limbs for building material. The smaller branches were thrown in a large brush pile that hid the mine entrance.

Sorting through the cut cedar, I spent two days building a sturdy corral next to where I planned to build the house. Having the horses and mules close to the house would make them harder to steal. Not too far in the future, I would work on fencing in the pasture, right now I just needed a corral.

Trimming posts and digging post holes was hard but satisfying work. I was building something that would last. That simple corral of indestructible cedar posts would still be there long after I died.

I awoke full of energy on my fourth morning at Lost Maples. In the invigorating January air, I again roamed up and down the canyons, identifying potential meadows and natural defenses.

Texas winters were more akin to fall in most places. The winter weather hovered in an in-between place where you neither sweated nor froze. Sure, there could be wild swings where it felt as hot as summer or you froze when a "northern" blew in. Such extreme weather rarely lasted more than three or four days.

Working in comfortable weather, by the end of the first week I had staked out the other forty-nine hundred acres with a pile of rocks every couple of hundred yards. I claimed portions of the bottom of the canyon at its widest and narrowest points. With carefully laid out corner stones, I laid claim to the grama meadow at the mouth of the canyon that ran in front of what would be my house. I calculated I was out of acreage when I claimed meadows on the tops of the two-thousand-foot-high mountains whose walls created my canyon. Strategic planning, that is what my pa called it.

In my second week at Lost Maples, I started building my house. Even though wood would have been easier, I chose to erect a stone building. I did not want someone burning down my home.

The house needed to provide protection and to disguise the mine entrance. My vision was to build a stone house big enough to cover the cave entrance and provide enough livable space until a bigger house could be erected next door.

I decided to build a rectangular house which would also make building a roof slanting in one direction easier. With long strides, I laid out a base that was twenty feet wide and thirty feet long. I used the logs to build a rock hauler and began to locate shale and limestone that would provide flat surfaces for stacking rock. Starting at one corner I began to lay one rock on top of another cascading off in two directions, it was like building a huge puzzle. By the middle of the week, I had two corners three feet high and five feet long in each direction.

Before I built any further it was important to build a cistern in the house's interior. Luckily, I had found a seep higher up on the hill. I intended to build a well at the seep, run the water down the slope to the house, and into a cistern where the water could be stored for any siege we might undergo. Plus, any time we needed water we would not have to climb the hill.

With defense in mind, I deliberately laid out the walls for the house on solid rock to prevent any Apaches from burrowing under and into the house. I did position one corner over dirt rather than stone. In the dirt portion of the floor, I dug down ten feet and laid rock with mortar to prevent any intruder from digging their way into the house. Next to the mortared wall, I laid out a well ten feet deep, three feet wide, and then added two more feet of height so that it extended two feet above the house's floor. I left a small opening entering and exiting the well, as well as a small opening in the house wall for the pipes I was going to insert.

To the mule's disappointment, I hooked him up to the rock hauler and headed to the hillside where I loaded up shale for the bottom and sides of the well. I spent the remainder of the day laying out the floor and sides of the well using generous slabs of mortar in between the rock.

Riding the mule to a spot a little over a mile away, I was able to get good quality clay out of a wet creek bank. Returning to the well, I lined the bottom and sides of the well with four inches of clay. I threw fire coals in the well to bake the clay and covered the opening. For two days coals were slowly fed into the well to keep up a constant low heat. After two days of baking, the indoor cistern was fire-hardened and would store enough water to allow us to survive any siege.

With the cistern completed, I built the other two corners of the house. In between the two corners, I laid the foundation for a hearth and chimney. The large chimney and cooking area were much bigger than needed, but since we needed to vent the air in the mine, the chimney could be used both for cooking and venting. Soon I had one complete wall with a chimney in the middle that was six feet wide.

On either side of the chimney, I began to build stone benches. Extending the full length of the wall on either side, the benches stuck out two feet and were eighteen inches tall. Once I framed the two rectangles on either side of the chimney, I mortared the rock tightly.

To most people, the benches would look like I cleverly built a rock seat for people to sit or a place to set cooking utensils. In reality, they were hiding places for gold.

Under a moonless night, I hauled gold bars up from the cave and stacked them inside the benches on both sides of the chimney. Then I poured sand into the benches until the gold was covered by several inches of sand. The next morning, I mixed mortar and laid rocks across the top of the benches. People sitting on the ledge next to the fire would never know they were sitting on a fortune in gold.

I even used gold bars to build the floor of the fireplace. The bars were laid side by side, four rows, twenty bars long, and ten bars deep. I covered them with sand and a layer of slate on top. The fireplace would contain gold bars for quick removal if ever needed.

Even after relocating gold to the benches and fireplace, the pit still contained three times as much gold as I removed. Being rich was complicated.

By the middle of the second month, the stone walls were three feet high. The presence of even partial walls was a relief. I needed protection not only from bad white men but also from Indians. The greatest threat was from the Comanche who raided in all directions from their strongholds in west Texas, north Texas, and the great expanse north of Texas. One always had to be watchful for the Apache raids from the south and west. Raiding parties occasionally showed up that were Kiowa and Tawakonis, and even some Wichita. There was even danger from renegades of tribes like the Cherokee and Choctaw fleeing hostilities in the east.

Though the walls were important, I needed to lay down a wooden floor. Most people would have thought me crazy to build the floor before I finished the walls, but I needed a floor to hide the cave entrance.

I worked hard splitting logs and facing them with my ax until they were relatively flat on two sides. In the end, I had a solid eight-inch-thick wooden floor, a sure sign of civilization in a land where many people had dirt floors. The floor planks had to be extra thick because I did not want anyone to hear a hollow echo if they walked over the concealed mine opening.

While I was admiring my newly finished floor, five Comanches rode up. The warriors were handsome men, tall, muscular, and self-confident. None of the Comanche had firearms, just bows casually held by their sides.

In broken English, they said they had ridden a long way and demanded I feed them. Most of the time if you respond passively to such a demand, the Indians will stalk into your house and take whatever they want. Some of the time, such a demand is a prelude to your murder.

The key was to remain calm and confident. I stood in the doorway of my unfinished house with my hand on my hip near my pistol. Without fear or hostility, in a commanding voice, I said, "Warriors need to hunt and feed themselves."

In response, one Comanche nudged his horse several feet in my direction. I assume he was the leader. He had a scar at the edge of his forehead, almost as if someone had tried to scalp him and stopped. Unlike the neutral faces of the other warriors, he bristled with animosity.

To Indians, a settler saying no was just the second step in a dance. The leader jumped off his horse and headed toward the unfinished house.

I immediately pulled my Colt and pointed it at him. With a smile, I pointed to the gun and said, "Five bullets, five dead Comanche."

Oh, that Comanche standing flat-footed twenty feet from me did not like that. He stopped in his tracks glaring at me. Just then an owl who had settled in the canyon behind the house began to hoot. Those Indians were riveted to the spot as they stared in the direction of the owl. Indians believe an owl warns of impending death.

Thanks to my great-grandmother, a sliver of the Irish ran through my blood. Like her, there were times when the veil opened, and I saw things for which I could not account. I pointed at the scarred warrior and said, "A woman will kill you."

That owl, my gun, and the potential shame of a warrior dying at the hand of a woman caused those Indians to glance nervously at one another. Turning his back to me, the Comanche remounted his horse. The warriors rode out, the air filled with war cries designed to intimidate me.

Lucky for me, the walls of my house were three feet high by now. On the side of the house where I had constructed my corral, I tied the mules and horses to the wall. Without a fire, I crept into a corner near the horses and prepared for a sleepless night.

In the middle of the night, I heard an eerie gurgle and a thud that could only be a hoof striking flesh. Several Indians rushed into the house seeking to locate my position. I opened up with my Colt, knocking two Comanche down as the third retreated over the three-foot wall. In the distance, I could hear one horse ride away.

I quickly popped a fully loaded cylinder into the Colt and changed positions. Though Woe snorted and pranced, I sat perfectly still, awaiting another attack. I knew I was a sitting duck if this was a large war party.

Half an hour later the sun peaked over the horizon illuminating what had unfolded during the night. Four dead Comanche lay on the ground, two killed by Woe. A warrior must have grabbed Woe's mane to leap onto his back. Woe reached around and ripped a four-inch hunk out of the Indian's neck. The eerie gurgle I had heard was the Comanche dying before he hit the ground.

The second Comanche must have misjudged where Woe was standing in the dark. Woe kicked out with the full force of his hindquarters. The Comanche caught a hoof dead center, crushing his chest, broken ribs shredding his heart and lungs.

My shooting had taken out the other two. The only survivor was the scarred warrior who had tried to enter the house the previous evening.

I knew Texans who would agree with me and many who definitely would not. But I buried those four Comanche on a nearby hill. I knew when the Comanche were able, they liked to bury their kin on high spots. I also anchored their weapons with rocks atop their graves so that you would know which Comanche was buried in each grave. Not sure why I did that, it just seemed the right thing to do.

From that day on, I worked like my tail was on fire, but I kept my eyes open. I needed my rock fortress. There was no telling when that Comanche or others might be back.

Despite the danger, I could not help but notice what a wonderful land I had settled upon. Throughout February, hawks of every type and size migrated north in kettles varying in number from dozens to hundreds.[1] They rode the air currents with little wing movement, traveling north in huge numbers before spreading out to spend the spring and summer alone or in pairs.

Ducks and geese of every size and color were migrating north. The geese occasionally stopped at one of the meadows to feed and were easy to pick off. Whether the geese were white, a mixture of white and black, or grey and black did not matter, they were a tasty break from venison. The ducks jammed in solid masses on any surface with water, and though easy to kill, were almost too beautiful with their shiny green heads and rainbow-like feathers.

Exploring the canyons in search of trees to cut, I looked with anticipation at the blooming persimmon trees and agarita bushes. Sweet meals were in my future.

By the end of the second month, I had three limestone walls one and a half feet thick and five feet high on three sides with no windows. The fourth side was primarily stone too, but in the stone, I used full-size tree trunks to build a frame on which I was going to hang doors large enough for two horses to walk through side-by-side. We needed such a large opening in case we needed to haul things in and out of the mine.

For the next stage, I wanted to build platforms elevated about five feet off the ground inside each corner of the house. I located a batch of oak trunks that grew relatively straight and trimmed them so that one side was flat. Starting at the narrowest part of each corner, I laid boards across the two walls, expanding out until I was using ten-foot lengths of timber. The result was elevated triangular platforms in each corner where people could sleep off the ground.

The corner platforms served a second purpose in that my intention was for people to store weapons in each corner. When attacked, we could stand on the wood platforms and fire down on any attackers through rifle ports. Since the planks were oak, with their dense grain they would last a long time and support significant weight.

Piling rock on the ground was the easy part. Lifting those rocks off the ground and hefting them into the air was an altogether different matter. I had to build walkways that even at an angle were painful as the walls grew taller.

One day when I was tired from hefting rock, it dawned on me to construct a pulley system to move the rocks from the ground to the top of the walls. The pulley connected to one of the mules made the work easier. I was glad no one had been around to watch me stupidly working myself to the bone.

With the corner platforms in place, I built the walls six feet higher all around for a total height of eleven feet. Into each corner, I built a slit two feet high and six inches wide that a rifle could fire down, left, right, or straight ahead. The field of fire was good for those in the house firing outward, but the narrowness of the slits reduced the danger to those in the house from outside fire. I also planned to build wooden shutters to cover each slit to keep out the heat, cold, rain, bugs, and critters.

After weeks of handling rock, my hands were a mess, but I felt content. I had four strong walls, four living areas off the ground, and a good field of fire. Several major tasks remained. I needed to build a roof and complete the well up the hill.

I built one length of the walls two feet higher than the other so that when the rain hit the roof it would flow down in one direction rather than two. To build the roof I simply had to cut enough twenty-foot timbers to go the thirty-foot length of the house. Each tree produced two three-foot-wide logs, so five trees were required for the roof alone.

In the evening I would sit on my growing walls and stare at the land around me. From my elevated perch, I marveled at the sea of bluebonnets that grew thicker every day in the meadow next to the house. After several weeks, the blue was crowded out by the red and orange flowers Professor Eldridge's book referred to as "Indian paintbrushes."

One morning in the middle of March, as I prepared my coffee, I gazed outside to see what looked like flowers in the meadow rising to fill the air. To my amazement, tens of thousands of butterflies filled the canyon and as one this brilliant, winged rainbow turned north. I had heard rumors that butterflies migrated like geese, but I never believed it and did not know anyone who had ever witnessed such a thing.[2]

NOTES

1. Travis Audubon, Jim Spencer, "What to Watch for in September: High-Flyers," accessed May 2, 2020, https://travisaudubon.org/uncategorized/September-bird-forecast-high-flyers. Every spring and fall, raptors migrate through Texas in large numbers, in some places, hundreds, thousands, and even tens of thousands can be seen daily. It is reported at Hazel Brazemore County Park in Corpus Christi, Texas you might see one hundred thousand migrating raptors in a day. For more information, contact Travis Audubon at www.travisaudubon.org or the Hawk Migration Association of North America at www.hmana.org.

2. Texas Butterfly Ranch (March 17, 2020), Monika Maeckle, "Monarch Butterfly Numbers Drop As Spring Migration Begins," https://texasbutterflyranch.com.

CHAPTER EIGHT

Screams jerked me out of heavy sleep. My first thought was Indians, again. I grabbed my Colt and peered around the corner to where the horses were staked out. In the moonlight, just outside the small corral, stood a large cougar whose shrieks sounded just like a terrified woman. Woe was rearing and stamping his hooves, momentarily keeping the cougar at bay.

I fired two shots in rapid succession. Unpleasant thumps indicated both shots were solid hits. The tawny cougar screamed, lurched ten feet, wobbled, and then collapsed. I heard several quick breaths and then the panting stopped.

With my foot, I prodded the cougar to be sure it was dead. Never one to put off a task, I built a large fire to provide enough light to skin out the cat and butcher the meat. Where I was from, cougar meat was preferable to venison.

Rolling the cougar's carcass over, I grimaced. The dead cougar was a nursing she-cat. In the morning I would have to back track the mama cat to put her kits out of their misery. Leaving the cougar's babies to slowly starve to death would be cruel.

I did not like killing creatures just because they were hunting for food. Even though it would be a lot of work, I was going to build a stone barn connected to the house so that the horses could be locked in at night. If the cougars, bears, and wolves could not get to the horses, I would not have to shoot them needlessly.

My uncle Jimmy taught me how to skin an animal and I did it with a great deal of skill if I say so myself. With patience and precise cuts, the pelt retained the tail, the paws, and even the ears and face of the cougar. Once the hide was scrapped and treated, I would place the pelt on the floor in front of the fireplace.

When the sun peeked over the horizon, I shouldered my rifle and began to backtrack the cougar. Thanks to a light rain during the night, dim paw prints were visible in the moist soil. Initially, the cat's trail was easy to find with a quick scan. Unfortunately, any time the cougar walked into an area where trees shielded the ground from the rain I lost her tracks. In those circumstances, I had to crisscross the area until I picked up her paw prints.

After a particularly frustrating attempt to pick up the trail, I looked up and the sun was directly overhead. I had been trailing the cat for six hours. What had probably taken the cat half an hour to walk, took me six hours to retrace.

I was a hard-headed person. When I started something, I stuck to it, even if it was a bad idea. My mother called this a good-bad trait.

Following the disappearing and reappearing tracks for another two hours, I found the cougar's den among boulders up the canyon wall. At the entrance, I built a smoky fire and waved the smoke into the den. Resisting the temptation to peer inside the den, I kept reminding myself to stand off to the side. The last thing I wanted was for some angry animal to roar out of the den and tear off my face.

Ten minutes passed, and nothing rushed out of the cave or even stirred. I crawled in with a torch in my left hand and my pistol in my right hand. The mama cat had been gone too long. Something had gotten in and killed her kits. Blood, guts, and small pieces of spotted fur were splattered all over the den.

With mixed feelings, I crawled out of the den. I was glad I did not have to kill the cougar's kittens, but it was sad to think they were killed while waiting for the mama I shot.

Melancholy settled over me as I sat down at the den's opening thinking about the death of the she-cat, her kits, and the long-dead miner. Life was hard and death was easy.

Looking out over the majestic canyon, dreary thoughts of death were pushed out by the beauty surrounding me. I found the sadness ebbing, replaced with gratitude. My new home was wild and beautiful. The deep blue sky reminded me of the ocean. Overhead, billowy white clouds shaped like mythical creatures raced across the sea of blue.

Trees of every kind stretched out across the horizon, their numbers and size dependent on the depth and quality of the soil, as well as the availability of water. With sufficient water and good soil, the oak, cypress, and cottonwood trees were ancient and so wide at the base that three men could not wrap their hands around the trunks.

Where the soil was thin, or the water sparse, spindly tree trunks were supported by twisted roots that tenaciously gripped the land. Even more impressive were the clumps of brush and cactus that somehow clung to precarious holds on the steep canyon walls.

Lush meadows popped up in surprising places, a testament to rich soil and unseen water. Delicate ferns feathered the canyon walls wherever a seep provided moisture.

The canyon echoed not only with the sound of rock slipping off the steep canyon walls, but also the chirp of birds in the bushes, trees, and even the walls themselves. Swallows darted through the air, chasing bugs for their young nestled in mud homes precariously suspended to the undersides of rocks thrust out dangerously from rock overhangs. Doves cooed contentedly as crows cawed, and blue jays screeched. Though they made no noise, occasionally a roadrunner with its head thrust forward would race across the canyon floor.

While gazing across the land, a faint mewing echoed off the canyon walls. I strained and walked toward the sound, but with every movement, the mewing stopped. Sitting down I waited ten minutes before the mewing started again. Quietly as possible, I moved toward the sound and the mewing stopped again. For an hour, this cycle repeated itself until I looked up and forty feet away saw a baby cougar clinging to the top of an oak tree. During the chaos of the den attack, the youngster must have escaped the cave.

My heart felt heavy because I did not want to kill this young cub that had miraculously survived. Standing at the bottom of the tree, I looked up, closely examining the kit. The little spotted fella looked to be about two months old. At six weeks the mama cat would have started introducing chewed-up meat into its diet. A chance existed, small that it might be, that the cat could survive off meat at this point.

Shielding my eyes with a hand, I stared up at the cub. He stared down at me and snarled. I burst out laughing. The little guy had spirit.

While traveling the mountain ranges out west, I encountered cougars who bore their young between April and August. In Texas, due to our mild winters, cougars could deliver any time of the year. For that reason, I was not surprised to see a kit that must have been born mid-January, shortly after I became a Lost Maples guest.

Delaying a difficult task never made it easier. Sighing, I grabbed a low-hanging oak limb and began to shimmy up the tree.

Bracing both my legs on a large limb, I positioned myself on the opposite side of the trunk from the cougar kitten. Taking a deep breath, I unbuttoned my jacket and adjusted my leather gloves. Holding one edge of the jacket, I threw the jacket around the opposite side of the tree so that it covered the entire kit. Before he could react, I wrapped him up like a papoose and jerked him away from the tree.

Oh, the kit was not happy. The violently thrashing ball of fur shrieked at the top of its tiny lungs. Every time the cat paused for breath, I pulled the coat tighter. After ten minutes of struggle, the coat was tight enough that the kit could no longer squirm. I removed three pieces of leather string from my front pocket and tightly tied all the loose ends of the coat into a neat package. Hopefully, I could safely carry the now whimpering kit down the tree with one hand.

Despite the chill in the air, by the time I climbed to the bottom of the tree one-handed I was sweating. If I had fallen out of the tree and broken a leg, I would probably have died there, all alone like the old miner.

Strangely enough, during the trek back to the house, the little cat did not snarl or squirm. After spending his whole life as part of a group with his mama and fellow cubs, I suspect he was bewildered at being alone. Even being with me was better than being alone. I shared his sentiments.

Back at the camp, I securely tied sticks together for a two-foot-by-two-foot square cage. I would keep the kit in the cage until he settled in and would not try to run away. Gently I placed my coat in the cage and secured the top to keep my ward from escaping. Through the wooden bars, I cut the strings binding him inside the coat. When the last string was cut, the coat plopped open, and the kit sat completely still, his eyes searching the unfamiliar surroundings.

The frightened cat and I stared at each other for ten minutes. Looking into the cat's deep blue eyes I softly apologized for killing his mama. I told him I could not make any promises, but I would do my best to take care of him.

When I was a kid, cougar cubs and their transformation fascinated me. Cougars' eyes are blue until about five months when the eyes darken to brown. Kits are born with tawny-colored skin and black spots. Around six months the spots begin to fade and are completely gone around two years.

Leaving the kit in peace, I went outside and began to lay out the walls for the stone barn on the side of the house with the big doors. At present, I had Woe, the two outlaw horses, and two mules. I suspected I would need space for far more than that in the future. Though not as big as the side door to the house, I planned on having a big exterior door the horses could enter and exit the barn. Both sets of doors would be barred from the inside to keep out marauding Indians and outlaws.

After several hours I returned to the cat. I untied the cage top and carefully lowered a small wooden bowl of water. Keeping an eye on me, the cat snarled and tentatively lapped at the water.

Suspecting my new friend was hungry, I got a piece of venison and chewed it into mush. In a second bowl, I lowered the mush into the cage. I was afraid the cat would reject the food just to spite me. Instead, the spotted kit walked up to the bowl and began eating the venison as though he had done so his whole life. This young cat's survival instinct was strong.

Our first week as companions, the cat alternated between snarling at me and missing me. One day he would snarl when I appeared, yet later in the day when I went to feed him, he would rub against the side of the cage and purr as though inviting me to touch him. I had a slashed finger to remind me that was a bad idea.

The effort took two weeks, but I added the rock barn and modified the house to connect with the barn. During the day, the horses and mules were either in the cedar corral or staked out in the grass. Before dusk, I locked them in the barn.

Building the rock barn turned out to be prudent. In the mornings it was not unusual to see predator tracks outside the barn. I saw cougar, bobcat, bear, and an occasional wolf track. With a bigger herd of horses, I could leave them in the pasture at night. A larger group of horses would present a formidable wall of kicks, bites, and sharp hooves.

My relationship with the kit changed when I finished tanning the she-cougar hide and set it in front of the fireplace. In a frenzy, the little kit tore at his cage to get out. He hurled himself with such ferocity against the stick cage I had to let him out before he could hurt himself. Upon his release, the mewing cat immediately went to the skin and rubbed his head all over his mama. I have to tell you, it broke my heart.

With his release from the cage, the contented kit spent his time laying on his mama and purring. He never tried to run away. I put food and water within easy reach and the kit ate or drank on his own schedule. For two weeks the freed kit was content to just lay on his mama.

Gradually the young cougar began to explore the house. Soon he was getting into things, batting stuff around the house and giving chase when it rolled away. After a month he would climb the ladder and sleep next to me in my bed, purring loudly like a clock. Being a man of little imagination, I named my cougar, Kit.

• • •

I got into the habit of sticking one or two of the outlaw rifles out of the rifle ports. This weapons display gave the appearance someone was always on guard and there was more than one of us.

One fine spring day two rough customers rode up to the house while I was out chopping firewood. Woe had warned me someone was near, so I wiped off my hands and placed one on my hip just above my pistol. I stood in the doorway where I could easily duck into the rock interior.

They stopped their horses thirty feet away and edged away from each other. "We are looking for an outlaw killer," one of them sneered.

Glancing up at the rifles I said, "The three of us don't know anything about that."

Both outlaws followed my glance upward and grimaced. Three against two, with two rifles already pointed at them were poor odds. With weak bravado, the one on the left with a patchy beard said, "If you see that outlaw killer you tell him we are looking for him."

I looked up at one of the rifles and called out, "Clem?" The outlaws looked up and while they were distracted I calmly palmed my pistol.

Staring expectantly at "Clem" and his rifle, they glanced back at me to discover I had them covered with my Colt.

With an animosity I did not fully feel, I barked, "Drop your rifles. Now." The scruffy outlaw on the left immediately threw his old flintlock Brown Bess down. The other outlaw leaned over and gently laid down what looked to be a percussion cap Kentucky long rifle.

"Since you gentlemen are looking for an outlaw killer, I am probably safe in assuming you are outlaws. I am a poor man and suspect if I killed you both right now I would collect a hefty reward. How much are you worth?"

Alarmed, the outlaws raised their hands and in squeaky voices said, "Now mister, there is no call for you to pull a gun on us."

"Sure there is, you are here looking to murder a man who kills outlaws. I don't know the fella, but I could use the money." Pointing my pistol to the guy on the left I said, "How much are you worth, one hundred, maybe two hundred dollars?"

Pointing to the outlaw relieved of the nice Kentucky rifle, I said, "Since you have done most of the talking, you must be the boss and worth the most. How much? Two or three hundred?"

Tilting my head up just a bit to the right, I yelled, "Clem when you shoot them don't injure the horses. That black is a fine animal."

Suddenly something got into Kit and he started wailing. Normally Kit just spent the daytime up in the loft sleeping and then roamed the house at night. For some reason, he was letting out a throaty scream.

"What is that?" a rattled outlaw asked.

"That is my brother Clem. He got shot in the throat once. I am the only person who can understand him."

Continuing to glance up at the rifle protruding from the window I yelled, "Yes Clem, Austin is a long way to haul dead bodies. I believe they would still give us the rewards if we just brought in the outlaws' heads. Hauling heads in a sack would be a sight easier than ferrying a couple of bloated bodies to Austin."

I pretended to drop my gun and those outlaws spurred their horses out of there as though lightning was flashing all around. Laughing, I watched them hightail it away. Dang, somehow word of my run-in with the outlaws had spread and now I was going to have to watch my back. I guess I should not be surprised word had spread. People like to talk. By the time the telling was told, I was probably famous for capturing a gang of ten and having only used one bullet to kill five of them.

Keeping an eye on the fleeing outlaws, I walked over and examined the guns they dropped. Every part of the Brown Bess was worn, the outlaw must have paid little for it or stolen it from a very poor man. The Kentucky rifle was clean and in good shape. The gentle manner in which the outlaw laid the gun down indicated he valued and took care of the gun.

I did not like taking their guns, but they came to kill me. Allowing them to hide in the brush and ambush me later that day was unwise. Now they would have to travel a distance to get a rifle or musket if they wanted to trade shots with me.

Kit was still screaming so I climbed up into the loft to see what had him so riled. I discovered he had flexed his front claws and hooked a claw on the blanket. No matter what he did, Kit could not shake the entangled blanket loose. Unhooking his claw, I hugged Kit and thanked him for his help.

In the house, I examined the guns closer. The Brown Bess was as worthless as I initially thought. The Kentucky rifle was in good shape and a percussion cap to boot. Most guns were flintlocks that relied on a piece of flint to strike steel and produce sparks to ignite a pan of gunpowder. Flintlocks had many downsides, with a failure to fire in damp weather the worst.

Percussion cap weapons avoided the flintlock's weakness. The small copper percussion cap possessed a mixture of powdered glass, fulminate of mercury, and chlorate of potash.[1] This cap was set on the nipple of an even smaller hollow tube that reached into the gun barrel. When the trigger hammer hit the cap, the cap detonated sending fire down the tube to ignite the gunpowder in the barrel.[2]

Texans are notorious for their ability to tell stories and argue. Outside of Indians and Santa Anna, Texans argued most passionately about anything related to weapons and percussion caps in particular. We argued about who created the first percussion cap, with assorted names and dates from 1814 to 1822 tossed about. When that argument lost steam we switched to arguing about when the first percussion weapons arrived in Texas. Then we jumped to violent arguments about how many percussion cap weapons were in Texas, with most agreeing the flintlock was more prevalent in 1836, but by 1840 percussions were becoming common.[3]

Though we Texans liked to argue, everyone agreed on the superiority of percussion over flintlock weapons. When a gun owner could afford to do so, flintlocks were converted to percussion caps.

• • • •

If we were going to have horses and cattle in Lost Maples, I needed to learn more about the meadows and possible pastures in the area. Using Professor Eldridge's book, I was able to identify a foot-tall grass already blooming and seeding in the meadows as buffalograss, a good source of forage. The currently blooming yellow indiangrass was already seven feet tall in some sections. Notes next to the drawing of the three-foot-tall sideoats grama indicated it bloomed in May and seeded in late summer to early fall. The professor noted that the three-foot-tall, little bluestem was nutritious in the spring, but less so as the year wore on.[4]

My land appeared to possess patches of healthy stands of forage for the animals. Unfortunately, as Dr. Eldridge pointed out, our area consisted of more canyons than meadows. We would have to seek out pastures further away and store forage to keep the animals close to the house.

The mesquite and cactus were in full bloom. Depending on the type of cactus, the blooms were bright red or brilliant yellow. Small pods protruded where the blooms dropped off the cactus. My mouth watered with the knowledge the pods would grow to the size of a man's thumb with twice the thickness. During May, the pods would turn deep purple and be as sweet as store-bought candy.

I awoke one mid-April morning to discover the blooms in the canyon filled with thousands of tiny hummingbirds.[5] Their brilliant red, green, and gold bodies blended with the blooms creating undulating waves of color.

For a week, my canyon was some kind of massive trail for migrating hummingbirds. I stopped trying to keep track of how many thousands of tiny bodies passed through my canyon each day. Suddenly one morning, they were gone. Not a single flower had a hummingbird bent in worship.

NOTES

1. Wikipedia, "Percussion Cap," accessed April 18, 2018, https://en.wikipedia.org/wiki/Percussion_cap.

2. Ibid.

3. Sons of the DeWitt Colony, John Bryant, "The Small Arms and Weapons of the Alamo Defenders," accessed April 3, 2018, http://www.sonsofdewittcolony.org/adp/history/1836/the_battle/the_weapons/small_arms.html.

4. Loflin and Loflin, *Grasses of the Texas Hill Country,* 35. The nutritional content of Texas grasses varies a great deal, as does the length of time the grass retains its nutritional content. Over time, some grasses lose their nutritional value and when cattle eat the grass they lose rather than gain weight.

5. Hummingbird Central, "Spring 2020 Hummingbird Migration Map and Sightings," accessed April 28, 2020, http://www.hummingbirdcentral.com. Many hummingbirds winter in Central America or Mexico. They migrate north through Texas from February to April, while the southward migration is from August to September.

CHAPTER NINE

In my fourth month at Lost Maples, April was fading, and May was peeking around the corner. In the distance, I observed a tendril of dust in the air typical of horses on the move. Comanche had been active in months past, but it was unlike the Comanche to foolishly warn people they were coming. I retreated to my house, barred the door, and laid out my guns.

Gazing out the narrow gun slots in my rock fortress, I watched the dust grow closer in a meandering manner as though searching for something. When the horses broke out of a grove of oaks, I heard a whooping as they raced toward me. No Comanche, but a sight for sore eyes. My brother Darryl, cousin Dennis, and good friend Kel galloped into sight.

Darryl was two years my junior, and in my eyes still a kid, a position he would argue vehemently against. He was twenty-two and we had been close our whole lives. Well, maybe not our whole lives. When Darryl was six, I took him out to the edge of our homestead and told him he was an orphaned Indian kid and needed to return to the Comanche. The look on Darryl's face pierced my heart. I never played a trick on him again and we had been best buds since.

My brother was the good-looking one in the family. All the girls loved Darryl. They were always finding some excuse to drop off a pie or some other baked good by the cabin to have a word with him. Even as a small child, grown women would pick up and hug Darryl. His attempts to wiggle out of their arms made for some embarrassing wardrobe problems.

My cousin Dennis and I had been like brothers since we were smallish critters. I was eleven months older, and Dennis felt a compulsion to compete with me. With Dennis, it was always who could throw a stick the greatest distance, carry the heaviest rock, hold their breath the longest, or stand closest to a snake? Our daily lives were a happy competition.

Kel and I were the same age. Well, practically the same age. He was seven days older. We had been friends since his folks moved down the prairie from us in 1828 when we were ten. Kel was the smart one in the group. He had a head for numbers and kept every penny he ever earned. Since Kel was also the strongest one of us, he tended to earn more when it came to field clearing, logging, or plowing.

Opening the front door, I lazily leaned out like I had not a care in the world. The boys rode up whooping and hollering. I just stared at them with bored droopy eyes.

Though the best educated and well-read of us four, I slipped into the casual speech we used with one another. "Wahl, just who might you three strangers be?" I asked, my words dripping with sarcasm.

"I sent word to kinfolks to come a running a while back. Who are you cowboys a-waltzing in here like you got all the time in the world to gallivant around? My message traveled roughly one hundred and sixty miles from Austin to Houston. I recollect it is a little under three hundred miles from Houston to here. I do believe, even if I was traveling on that crowbait sorrel of Dennis', I could still make it under twenty days, even walking that crippled-up-looking horse. Here it is, almost four months later."

Turning to my brother Darryl I said, "Who is this that comes riding up on an Appaloosa that shouts, 'Look at me. I am a tenderfoot. My white horse with big brown spots does not blend in and I sure can't hide. All you wild Indians come kill me.'"

Instantly they switched from slouching to sitting straight up in their saddles and puffed out their chests like they were insulted. Dennis said, "Your chicken scratching of a message took six weeks to travel from Austin to San Antonio, Houston, Waller, and on to Darryl. When the letter arrived, Darryl was down in New Orleans. Another month passed before Darryl returned to Texas."

I felt chastised until I added up all the weeks. "I sent that message sixteen weeks ago. If it took Darryl ten weeks to get the message, where have y'all been for the past six weeks?"

They looked taken aback. Dennis somewhat sheepishly said, "Now it's true, that we encountered some enticing little streams on the way here. It just seemed criminal if we did not stop to catch ourselves a nice batch of catfish and perch once or twice."

Kel responded with, "Now Rye, you know how I love to hunt. When I saw those huge bear tracks, I had to chase that monster down, even if it did take the best part of a day. Then there was that time we flushed a flock of fat turkeys that scattered for miles."

Darryl was huffing and puffing, "Now Rye, you know what a gentleman I am. When I saw that beautiful little straw-haired girl at that German farm on the way here, we just had to stop and offer to help them cut some wood. They sure seemed short-handed, with only five girls in the family, and no young men to help them. Course, that help turned into three days. In the end, we had to escape in the middle of the night. That stern old German farmer would have married us off to three of them fillies and made indentured servants of us all."

When I started laughing they knew I was not mad. All three jumped down from their horses and piled on top of me like we did when we were kids. After rolling them off we just stood staring at one another, what a grand adventure this was going to be.

CHAPTER TEN

Having put away their horses and stowed their gear, we gathered inside the stone house. Dennis who was the recognized expert at building back in Brenham, walked around grunting approvingly at the stonework and floor. Kel, who was the best woodsman among us, praised the narrow slits I built to create a defensive field of fire. I pointed to the elevated platforms in each corner and explained that they should find a corner they wanted to claim for sleeping and to store their gear.

Without being told, Kel, Dennis, and Darryl began to organize personal armories on their selected platforms. Soon each corner had a row of rifles and muskets laid out, along with assorted shotguns, pistols, and even a long knife or two. Next to each weapon was the required ammunition for the gun.

Texas was a confluence of weaponry. From the south, there were weapons from Spain and Mexico. French weapons via Louisiana flowed into Texas through trade and travel. Thanks to the American neighbors to the east, American-designed and British redesigned weapons poured into Texas.

Since most guns were single shots, out of self-protection people tried to collect as many weapons as possible. The most common weapons were muskets, followed by rifles, with more of the long guns owned than pistols.

Collecting whatever weapons came your way was a problem because you also had to find ammunition. Not only did the guns vary in caliber from .32, .45, .50, .58, .60, to .75, but the gun caliber might vary with use. Once a barrel became fouled, it was not unusual to have to bore out a gun's barrel to a larger caliber. Gun swapping was common as people tried to reduce the number of different types of ammunition they had to carry for their guns.

Besides caliber, there was the problem of whether you could find paper cartridges for your gun. If you could not, then you had to carry a powder horn and lead balls. The advantage with paper cartridges was that reloading was much faster, and you always ended up with the same amount of powder firing your lead.

The percussion cap weapons did introduce a new problem. If you used caps, you had to worry about running out of caps to fire the gun.

Fortunately for us, Kel came from a gun family. They had enough weapons to arm a militia. When you walked into Kel's house, the number and beauty of the guns were dazzling.

Every member of Kel's family, including his sister, was taught how to repair and manufacture guns. With the production of percussion caps, Kel became an evangelist and constantly harangued us to buy any caps we encountered.

Having set up their weapon stations, everyone began a more detailed exploration of the house. Kel immediately noticed I had started a small library. Walking over to where I had built a small bookcase that contained a dozen books, Kel nodded approvingly. "I see you are still reading. Rye, I never knew anyone who enjoyed reading as much as you do. You have collected some leather-bound books since I last saw you."

Smiling, I said, "Yep, I picked up the leather-bound books in California." Pointing to several worn-out books with severely tattered pages, I said, "The paperbacks were traded around campfires in some pretty desolate places."

With embarrassment, I said, "Other than that bookcase, I have not had time to build any chairs or furniture of any kind, so please sit on the ledge I built by the fireplace."

"Boys, I need for you to be completely honest with me." I looked each one sternly in the eye.

"Did you tell anyone you were coming to see me because I found gold? You must be honest. If you did, our lives are in danger, and we need to take precautions."

Kel, Darryl, and Dennis examined each other closely. "Nope," each exclaimed out loud.

"Ok, I believe you. Once word gets out we have discovered gold, people will come running to take our gold, land, and lives. We have a lot to accomplish before the news about our gold gets out."

"First, we need to build a channel to run water from the rise above us into the cistern here in the house. To keep the house from getting flooded, we need to run the overflow to a holding pond a short distance from the house. We can enclose the holding pond in a pasture that can also be used to water the horses and keep them close to the house."

"Second, we need to build a bigger house next to this one that we can all live in comfortably and defend. This new home needs to be connected to this house and I will explain why in a moment."

"Third, we need to create a decoy mine about a half-mile from the real mine. That way if some crooked politician tries to steal our mine, he steals something worthless."

"Fourth, we need to stack stones all along the border of our land to clearly show the boundaries. I hope you boys have already been to Austin to claim land around here."

Darryl burst out laughing and while guffawing said, "Actually we took so long to get here because we have been scouring the land for Independence Vouchers. Many Texas families have been offered five to ten percent on the head for the land vouchers, so they just put them away and forgot about the vouchers. We told folks if they gave them to us, we would pay one hundred percent of the value within a year. No rock was left unturned as we searched high and low for vouchers to expand our acreage."

With low expectations, I asked, "How much land did you get?"

Kel replied, "I have my Bounty grant for 1280 acres, the First Class Headright is 1,476 acres, and two Donation grants for 640 acres each totaling 4,036 acres. Dennis has the same amount. Darryl's total is 640 acres larger because of the Bounty grant with your dad dying in the war. In all, we started with 12,748 acres."

"We found eight folks like you and Darryl who were in Texas by March 4, 1836, fought in the war, participated in two of the Donation grant battles, and lost their fathers. That is 4,676 acres times eight which equals 37,408 acres. We found ten men like Dennis with land vouchers for 4,036 acres that when totaled together added another 40,360 acres. Five widows entrusted us with their land vouchers for an additional 23,025 acres. Then we pulled together our money and bought another 1,459 acres. When you add your five thousand acres to our land, the total is one hundred and twenty thousand acres."

My loud whoop reverberated off the stone walls. "Boys, we are set," I yelled. "After building the water system, a second house, a decoy mine, and our outer boundary line, we will be ready for phase two."

"We have to time phase two right. Before anyone knows we have gold, Kel and Darryl must return home and pay those twenty-three people the full value of the vouchers they entrusted to you. Even more importantly, you must get a signed receipt."

"Upon your return home, this must be done as quickly as possible to prevent people from holding out on us. If they do, then act like you are going to give them their paper back and ride away. I suspect the possibility of that gold leaving will motivate them to stick to the deal. By splitting up, you can complete the voucher paybacks twice as fast. See if you can each hire a man we know from home to accompany you around. You don't want to get robbed traveling around with all that gold."

"Kel and Darryl, even if it's family, don't tell anyone where the gold came from or that you are headed to Austin. I do not want you boys to get bushwhacked. Nor do we want a gang of outlaws rushing to Lost Maples while we are in Austin."

"We will give you travel time and two days to hand out the gold. I will try to time it so we three arrive in Austin on the same day. At that point, we need to take some of the gold and open accounts in several different banks. Too many banks are failing these days, so we need to make sure one bank failing does not destroy us."

"Once the accounts are opened with gold, the rush will begin. I will immediately go to the land office and buy as much land as the remaining gold we have with us allows. I suspect we can double our acres which should create even more space between us and everyone else. Yes, I know it is a lot, but I do not want to risk someone claiming there was a land office mistake, and our land is west of our mine. I figure if we buy all the land around our canyons there is no way they can say the survey lines are wrong."

"Plus, mining gold is no way to live. We have always dreamed of having a ranch. I would have to say one hundred and twenty thousand acres is a good start."

"Kel, when the time comes, you will draw up some legal documents and get them notarized by a lawyer and filed in the Republic's Archives Office. Darryl will load up with supplies at the mercantile."

Being the more practical one among us, Kel asked, "Where will we get all this gold you keep referring to?"

Smiling, I said, "We already have that much gold. I will come back to that."

"I did not hear my name," said Dennis with a pout on his face.

"That is because you have the most important job of us all," I said with a stern look.

"Your job will be to guard the mine. I want you here in case word gets out gold has been discovered in Lost Maples before we get back."

"I will ride hard for the mine once I buy the additional acres. Kel and Darryl should be six days behind with the wagon. Until then Dennis, our future rests in your hands."

CHAPTER ELEVEN

"Let's talk about our land. I want to avoid any future fights over ownership. Kel, who is the smartest of us four, will write up legal papers in which we all agree the original five thousand acres I started with is mine only. Each of you will likewise own five thousand acres in your name."

"Kel will write up a second document in which the remaining land will be shared jointly by the four of us. The joint ranch is currently one hundred thousand acres. By the time we are finished, our shared ranch will be much larger than that."

"A joint bank account will be opened to fund the running of the jointly owned ranch. No one can sell the jointly owned land. When a partner dies, the heirs must keep the land or sell it back to the joint ranch."

"Now about the gold. I found it. To avoid any future fights over ownership, I will retain full ownership of the mine and the gold. You will have to trust me to share it with you. Not because I am legally obligated, but because I want to share the gold."

Dennis did not intend to sound disagreeable, but said, "What if my land or the joint land has a gold mine on it? I would like to have a mine all my own."

I smiled at Dennis, "I understand and respect whatever you decide. Y'all know little gold has ever been found in Texas. I strongly suspect my gold mine is the only one in the area. You are welcome to try your luck on your land, but this is a one-time offer."

Dennis asked, "Is there any chance this is Jim Bowie's Lost Silver Mine?"

I shook my head irritably. Dennis had a fascination with everything related to Jim Bowie. "First of all, I found a gold mine, not a silver mine. Second, Bowie's mine is rumored to be one hundred miles north of us on the San Saba River or one hundred and twenty miles northeast of us on the Llano River. Third, let me emphasize the word rumored, as in a fairy tale. Bowie looked for that mine in 1831 and 1832 and never found it."[1]

Dennis took offense at being so roundly chastised, so he picked a fight he thought he could win. Sarcastically he said, "I guess you don't believe Jim Bowie's brother Rezin forged the first Bowie knife out of a meteorite?"[2]

Shaking my head, I said, "That is another fairy tale. Do you know how hard it would be to forge anything out of a meteorite? By the way, Rezin designed the knife, and the Louisiana blacksmith Jesse Clift made the knife."[3]

Kel held up his hands, "Enough with this pissing contest. Can we get back to our mine and the gold you said already exists?"

Unwilling to give up, Dennis mumbled, "Well, there is no denying Bowie was a smuggler with Jean Laffite."

Laughing, I just shook my head. Smiling at Dennis and the others, I said, "Gentlemen, you asked if we have enough gold." Walking over to a box in the corner, I reached in and pulled out a bag, and untied the strings. For maximum effect, I slowly poured out the gold-veined quartz as they gasped.

"I have ten bags just like this one. Each of you will receive ten percent of what has already been mined."

Casually I tossed Kel, then Dennis, and finally Darryl, a bag of gold. "You each get one bag and I get the other seven."

With trembling fingers, they untied the strings and poured chunks of translucent crystal heavily veined with gold into their hands. Watching with satisfaction, I continued, "That ore is from the walls of the gold mine."

Glancing at their feet, I said, "I built this house on top of the mine so that no one will ever know where it is located."

"See that little room over there? In that room, I built wooden shelves that swivel out to reveal the gold mine entrance which is a crack in the ceiling of a cave. You need a ladder to climb down into the mine. That room will be my bedroom so nobody else should be entering it."

"In this house, we need to build a second room that is locked. We will tell people it is where we store our processed gold. Someone may eventually get in and steal whatever gold we have stored, which will not be much. They will never know the gold's source."

With a huge smile on my face, I walked over to the fireplace, dug around in the ashes, and extracted a dull bar. "In addition to the ten percent each of you gets of the raw gold I have already found, you will get ten percent of the refined Spanish gold I discovered."

I wiped the ashes off the bar and with a dramatic flourish laid the gleaming gold bar at their feet. Smiling, I added, "I also found a five-foot-deep pit filled with gold bars. By my calculation, each small bar weighs roughly five to six ounces. The bigger bars weigh ten to twelve ounces. To be conservative, if the small bar weighs five ounces, at $18.93 per ounce that would be almost one hundred dollars each. The bigger bars would be worth twice as much. If you agree to my terms, each of you will start with one hundred thousand dollars in gold."

A hush descended on the room as everyone held their breath. Exhaling as one, they stared as though in a dream.

"I can live with that deal," said Dennis.

"Yep, sounds fair to me," gulped Darryl.

"No problem with that," smiled Kel.

Thus, was born the Rattlesnake Mine, co-owned from the start by four very lucky young Texans.

NOTES

1. Handbook of Texas Online, William. R. Williamson, "James Bowie," accessed May 3, 2020, https://tshaonline.org/handbook/online/articles/fb045. Though Menard, Texas has taken credit for the location of the Jim Bowie Lost Silver Mine, the exact location has never been definitively identified.

2. Texas Hill Country, Llyod Tackitt, "The Billion Dollar Lost Mine of the Hill Country," accessed May 3, 2020, https://texashillcountry.com/billion-dollar-lost-silver-mine-hill-country/.

3. Handbook of Texas Online, William. R. Williamson, "Bowie Knife," accessed May 5, 2020, https://tshaonline.org/handbook/online/articles/lnb01.

CHAPTER TWELVE

Brimming over with excitement to see the gold mine, the boys could not settle down and restlessly stalked the floor. Finally, I told them, "Yep, there is gold right under our feet. Unfortunately, there is also a huge nest of rattlers, but probably no more than sixty or seventy of them. Of course, the one I killed when I found the mine was seven-foot-long and as thick as my wrist."

Pointing to the fireplace I said, "The skin is nailed over the mantle." Like a trio of owls sitting on a fence, their heads swiveled to the fireplace. Their eyes widened as they settled on the huge rattler's skin stretching the full length of the mantle.

"I recommend we don't go down to the mine until we have a plan for removing all the snakes. What do you think?"

"We must go down into the dark mine knowing it is full of snakes?" asked Darryl.

Staring at me, they waited for an indication I was kidding. When they saw I was not kidding, flashes of horror crossed their faces and intensified as they recognized the terror in each other's faces.

"We must go down into the darkness knowing it's full of snakes?" Darryl asked again.

"Well no, you drop a ladder down, then you very slowly climb down swinging a torch to make sure there are no snakes at the base of the ladder. Sticks are spread out on the floor, so be sure you pay attention to whether you are looking at a snake or a stick. When you get to the bottom, do not get upset if you see someone staring at you. It is just an old miner who got bit by one of the rattlers."

Their faces could not have been more horror-stricken. Looking at each other, they turned their attention to me, staring at me like I had lost my mind.

With a dead pan face, concealing the delight I was experiencing at their discomfort, I said, "See, there was this old fella who found the mine in 1834. Dan, that was the miner's name, got bit and broke his leg trying to get away. Or maybe he broke his leg and then got bit by a rattler. Anyway, Dan left a note saying whoever found him could have the mine if they killed the rattler and left him sitting there. I killed and ate that big old rattler, then I left the man in peace where he was." This explanation seemed to further horrify my companions.

"Let's not worry about sightseeing around the mine until we have a rattler plan." They nodded in agreement.

"Tomorrow we will start by digging a well."

• • •

Being used to taking care of ourselves, we fell into old patterns for preparing dinner. Kel had shot several rabbits shortly before arriving. Quickly skinning the rabbits Kel handed them off to Dennis who dipped them into some weird concoction that was supposed to give them flavor. Darryl was busy building a fire and soon the smell of roasting rabbits filled the air.

Everyone was sitting in front of the fireplace watching the rabbits cook, when Kel who had the best hearing said, "What is that?"

We stopped what we were doing and listened. A light scratching at the door was followed by a faint scream. Standing suddenly, I moved as far away from the door as possible and wheezed, "It's that dead miner, he comes to the door every night."

Kel, Darryl, and Dennis looked at my pale face and wide eyes. My hands began to shake. We played jokes on each other all the time and I could see they were struggling with whether to believe me.

Suddenly, Dennis pulls out his pistol and moves toward the door. "Ghost, or not, I am going to fill him with holes."

Alarmed, I grabbed Dennis and said, "Stop, I was just kidding. Don't shoot, that is my friend Kit."

I opened the door and said, "Come on in Kit."

Kel, Darryl, and Dennis would have been less shocked to see the dead miner. What they saw, was a four-month-old cougar saunter into the house. Kit walked right up to the roasting rabbits, sat down, and stared at the cooking meat.

Reaching in, I cut off a piece of rabbit and laid it down in front of Kit, and warned, "Watch out now, it's hot."

Dennis was the first to speak. "What the hell?"

"Boys, I would like to introduce you to my friend Kit. He moved in with me a little over a month and a half ago."

Kel knelt and rubbed Kit between the ears. Kit looked up at Kel and just climbed into his lap. Kel said, "Wahl Rye, we sure are glad to meet your girlfriend."

With a confused look, I stared at Kel.

With a look of disgust, Kel said, "Why you stupid country bumpkin, this is a she-cat, not a he-cat."

My little joke on the boys had turned on me. To salvage some of my pride I said. "Out of respect for Kit, I never went looking between his legs. Kel, only a dirty old cowboy like you would do such a thing."

• • •

The next morning with Kit dutifully following us, we walked out the door and headed up the gentle slope to the water seep. I had previously dug out some of the rock and dirt creating a pool one foot deep by one foot wide. Kel looked down and commented, "That is clear-looking water." Dipping a hand into the small pool, he brought it to his lips and smiled, "Tastes fresh and sweet too."

Dennis was the builder among us. His praise meant something when he said, "That is a nice little pool you created. What we need to do is to deepen it as far down as possible. When crossing Can Creek I noticed there was some thick cane growing. We can cut the cane in twenty-foot lengths, split it lengthwise, hollow out the cane, and then wrap wet leather every six inches that when dry will tighten that cane into an indestructible pipe."

"We need to start that pipe at about two feet below the surface of the well, dig a trench two feet deep, and run that pipe underground until till we get to the house. With a little work, we can chisel out a small circle in the exterior rock wall you built under the cornerstone of the house. Then we will cut a similar small hole in the cistern for the pipe to come through the clay cistern into the house. At the top of the cistern, we place another pipe that runs into a trough in the barn. Another stretch of pipe can run from the trough to a small dam we will create to the left of the house. Here the dammed water can be stored up and used to irrigate the pasture and a garden."

Dennis pointed at Darryl and Kel, "The three of us will return to Can Creek and cut cane. Rye you seem to be the rock expert around here. While we are gone, why don't you start hauling some rock for the dam."

"Dammit Dennis. See that house there, I have been hauling rocks for weeks."

With a laugh, Dennis responded, "Yep, you ought to know exactly where to get the good rock." I sighed and nodded my head in resignation.

Dennis, Darryl, and Kel headed to the creek and I rode to the cliff where some manageable stone lay. By the time the boys returned with their large haul of cane, I had made three trips with stone.

Spreading the cane out, we set to work splitting the cane which was four inches in diameter and mostly hollow. Every ten to twelve inches we took out our knives and removed a quarter-inch thick membrane that separated the bamboo segments. With an hour of daylight left, we had a pile of bamboo ready to serve as our pipe.

I turned to Kel, already knowing the answer. "In the morning, do you think you can find some game whose hide we can cut into leather strips to bind the pipe?"

Kel grinned, "While cutting the cane I saw deer tracks. One deer should provide plenty of binding."

Talking about the deer it dawned on us that we had not eaten all day. "Being rich is a great way to lose weight," said Dennis. "You get too excited to remember to eat."

With a smile and a shrug, I said, "Boys, thanks to that old trapper I have cans of beans for all those who can wait for venison until tomorrow."

CHAPTER THIRTEEN

Long before the first rays of the sun graced the world, Kel quietly gathered up his rifle, pistols, and knives, slipping out of the door without awakening anyone. Uncharacteristically, the rest of us laid in bed until the sun peeked over the horizon. Reluctantly we crawled out of our comfortable blankets, boiled a pot of coffee, and then grabbed an assortment of tools. We laid out our line from the well to the house and started digging. When Kel trailed in two hours later with a velvet horned four-point buck we had the rough outline of a trench from the house to the well.

Kel proceeded to skin the deer and nailed the hide on a wooden frame. Normally Kel would spend a week scrapping and soaking the hide. Since we were just looking to cut the hide into leather strings, Kel scrapped the meat off the hide and then rubbed on some foul mixture of urine, salt, and deer brains.

Darryl and Dennis butchered the buck while I roasted the liver, heart, and small chunks of meat in a pan. The gentle breeze was blowing west to east and must have carried the scent of cooking venison on the breeze. I was cooking my second pan when I saw movement out of the corner of my eye. Looking up I expected to see Kit waiting for food. Instead, three Indians were squatting on the ground fifty feet away staring at the meat.

With a single glance, I immediately knew they were not Comanche. For Comanche never seemed to leave their horses, and when they did, they squatted awkwardly as if eager to return to their animals. The comfort with which these three squatted was reassuring. We wanted nothing to do with the Comanche.

Holding up my hand in the universal sign of greeting I grunted my standard Karankawa for hello. I motioned toward the pan to indicate sharing. Kel was still scarping the hide, but he was now scraping at the side of the hide where his rifle leaned against the house. Just above and to the right of me I saw a rifle barrel peeking out of one of the rifle ports. That left only one of us unaccounted for during this potentially deadly situation.

Suddenly, Darryl came waltzing around the corner, walks up, takes the pan right off the fire, and saunters up to the Indians. He placed the pan with the half-cooked meat on the ground in front of them, reaches in to grab a hot chunk of venison, and motions for them to take a piece. With a glance at each other, the Indians grabbed a piece of sizzling meat with their fingers and started eating.

When the pan was empty, our visitors began to talk. The three Karankawa were out hunting an hour east when they saw two dozen Comanche. They immediately stopped hunting and were headed back to their camp when they smelled the meat. With a mixture of sign language, English, and Karankawa they indicated their camp had been reduced to a handful of people.

The past ten years had been hard on their group. The Mexican Army had crossed the lands they lived in four times in the last ten years, killing everyone they saw each time. Whenever portions of the Texas Army crossed their lands, any Indians that survived the Mexican Army were chased and killed. After the Texas Revolution, any survivors were savaged by the Apache, and even more so by the ever-marauding Comanche.

Darryl indicated his understanding. Returning to the fire he grabbed a quarter section of the deer and walked back to the Indians. Handing them the meat, Darryl flashed the sign for goodbye and returned to the fire with the pan.

When the Karankawa were gone, Darryl related his conversation with the Indians. The reactions around the fire were mixed. Kel was a hunter and admired the abilities of the Indians. Darryl had the kind of disposition where he always got along with everyone. Dennis on the other hand hated Indians. He believed Texas was for Texans and all Indians should be forced to leave or be killed.

My view was more complex. I saw them as individuals, some kind and some cruel. Whether I accepted or killed them depended upon their behavior.

Considering the Karankawa had no reason to lie about the presence of Comanche, it was agreed we would only work in pairs and no one should go anywhere or do anything alone. Caution would slow down our work, but it was better to be careful than dead.

Around the fire that night, Kel related the latest he knew about the Indian troubles. Back in January, the Comanche sent the Republic a message they were tired of war and asked for a peace conference. The Texans set up a peace meeting at the Council House in San Antonio. On March 19, 1840, twelve Comanche chiefs arrived at the meeting with their warriors and families to negotiate.[1]

Three months earlier when first approached about peace talks, the Texans laid out the condition the Comanche had to bring all their white captives to the talks. The Comanche showed up with only one white captive. The enraged Texans told the Comanche they would be held prisoner until they brought in all their other captives.

Hearing the sacredness of the peace meeting was broken, the Comanche tried to fight their way out of the packed Council House. In their attempt to escape, thirty-five of the sixty-five Comanche were killed, along with seven Texans who mainly died from shooting each other.[2]

Chief Buffalo Hump was reported to be recruiting warriors to exact revenge for what became known as the Council House Massacre. He was clamoring for the three dozen different Comanche bands spread across the southwest to join him in making war on the whites. The opportunity to make peace with the Comanche was lost.

Kelly ended with a warning. "We need to keep alert. The Council House Massacre was four weeks ago. We know the Comanche will strike back, we just don't know when or where."

NOTES

1. Wikipedia, "Council House Fight," accessed April 10, 2018, https://en.wikipedia.org/wiki/Council_House_Fight.
2. Ibid.

CHAPTER FOURTEEN

Thin wet leather strips were wrapped around the bamboo pipe. Given that it was a dry day, the raw leather would shrink and harden in the sun. By the end of the day, the leather would be as hard as an iron hoop.

Dennis looked at Kel, "You are the strongest, can you get some of those mining tools and dig or smash enough rock to deepen that seep well. If you can go deeper, that is even better. I will try to dip out the water while you dig."

Watching Dennis pour out the dipped water, a thought hit me. I said, "Dennis when you dip that water, pour it into the trench as we dig to soften up the ground."

With the ground damp, digging was easier, and we made quick progress. In between letting the water soak into the trench, Darryl and I began to haul rocks for the well and the dam. After two rock hauls taking roughly three hours, we checked on Kel. To our amazement, the well was already five feet deep. With just the top of his shoulders and his head visible, Kel yelled, "How deep do you think we should go?"

Bending over and looking down in the hole I said, "Not much more."

Kel smiled, "Rye, why don't you haul up some flat rock that I can use for the well foundation. I will stop digging when you get back."

Sighing deeply, I walked down the slope, grabbed one of the mules, and Darryl and I went down to the shale outcropping. Carefully examining all the rocks, I only selected the rocks with flat tops and bottoms. By the time an hour had elapsed, I returned to find Kel was now standing in a seven-foot-deep well.

Dennis looked exhausted. Since it was early May, the nights, evenings, and mornings were pleasant, but during the heat of the day, one's clothes would drip with sweat during hard labor. Dennis had a bucket on a rope and was hauling water as it seeped into the well. Fortunately, the seep was slow to fill, but it was exhausting work in the heat all the same. We took turns dumping the buckets of cool water in the trench and on ourselves.

Carefully, we lowered the rocks in a rope sling and Kel began to build the foundation. He built the well bottom three layers of rock deep and laid the first circle of rocks for the well walls. Steadily laying rock in an ever-rising circle, Kel stopped when he got within two feet of the surface. At that point, we inserted the cane pipe and mortared it tight.

When Kel reached the top of the well, he extended the walls two feet higher than the surrounding landscape. We did not want dirt and debris to flow down the hillside and into our clean well. Working with efficient motions, we shoved mortar between all the rocks.

Fortunately, the seep filled slow enough that with a little manpower, the mortar could be kept dry before the water level climbed up the well wall. With Kel in the bottom scooping up water with a bucket, and the three of us pulling up and emptying each bucket, we were able to keep the mortar dry for the next four hours. In the heat, the mortar dried and hardened quickly.

With the well completed, we built a wooden lid to cover the top of the well. After covering the opening, we sloped dirt down the sides of the two feet of rock thrusting up from the ground so the well looked like a small natural mound. We piled brush on top and erased any evidence this was our water source. No one could stop or foul our water if they did not know where it originated.

Meanwhile, Darryl and I connected the bamboo pipe the entire distance to the house. For the time being, we left the pipe uncovered so that we could find and correct any leaks.

After laying pipe to the house, we laid the bamboo pipe from the house to the barn. From the barn, we ran the pipe to the top of the pasture where it would water the grass as it rolled downhill to accumulate at the dam.

In the fading light, Darryl and I grinned at one another. Though we had worked at an exhausting rate from sunrise to sundown, we had accomplished a lot. We had a seven-foot-deep well, a twelve-foot-deep house cistern, and a dammed area that would hold a half-acre of water. In a land of scarce water, we would be water-rich.

•   •   •

When we awoke the next morning, it was to find Indians at the dam. The three Karankawa from yesterday were accompanied by four squaws and three scrawny kids, a three-year-old girl, a six-year-old boy, and what was probably a twelve-year-old boy.

Darryl went down the slope to investigate. After a long parlay, Darryl returned looking a little sheepish.

"Um, uh, seems the Karankawa are afraid of the Mexicans, Texans, Apache, and especially the Comanche. Yesterday every direction they went, they saw signs of Comanche. The Karankawa want to know if they can camp on our land for a short time."

"Aw, Darryl, you soft-hearted corn pone," growled Dennis. "I ain't sharing my land with no Indians."

A long and at times heated discussion ensued. In the end, everyone, even Dennis, agreed having extra sets of eyes watching for Comanche and bad white men might work to our advantage. Darryl walked down the slope and told the Karankawa they could stay, as long as they camped down the slope from us. Hopeful his message was getting through, Darryl then cautioned them about not fouling the dammed area with urine and shit since we were going to store water and pasture our horses by the dam.

If the Indians were going to remain in our area, I did not want them killing Kit. I asked Darryl to call all the Indians up to the house. When they arrived, I walked out the front door with my fingers gripping the red bandana around Kit's neck. I needed to address the issue of Kit's safety in a way that would be understood by the Karankawa.

With Darryl translating, in a quiet voice, I said, "This is my spirit animal. Treat her with respect. If you attempt to kill or harm her, your own spirit animal will abandon you."

Staring out over the Karankawa, I scratched Kit's favorite spot behind her left ear. In pleasure, Kit let out a wail that nailed down my warning. The frightened look on every face confirmed no one would try to harm Kit.

With enthusiasm, I turned to the boys and said, "All right, let's get our house built." The groans that met my greeting were not encouraging. I could not blame them. To build a home would require a lot of work, but the building would go quicker with four people.

• • •

Since it was spring, while locating rock and timber for the new house we kept our eyes out for things to eat. On the edge of forests, we found plump blackberries clinging to long thorn-covered stems. In the meadows, we encountered wild onions, dandelions whose green leaves you could eat, and pigweed that if soaked first was edible. Every cactus we encountered was closely examined for the dark purple plums whose soft squishy interior was sweet when ripe.

Hauling rocks and logs for a week, we had enough raw material to start building the new house and enough wild greens for every meal. Working non-stop for two weeks, the four of us erected a stone structure forty feet long and twenty-five feet wide whose height and build were like my home. Unlike my house, theirs had a stone floor rather than wood. They had a cistern, but only five feet deep.

After splitting and surfacing the longest logs, we threw a loop over them and the mules pulled the logs up the sides of the building to the roof. Maneuvering the unwieldy logs into place was dangerous and frustrating. Everyone was in a foul mood by the end of the day.

"Damn them Indians. They have been sitting and watching us work for three weeks without an offer to help," complained Dennis.

"Now Dennis, those Indians know we aren't building them a house. How can you expect them to join us in this back-breaking work? Anyway, squaws build their houses, not the men," said Darryl. "Those Indians over there can put up and dismantle their homes in an hour, so which of us is smarter?"

"I bet if you and those Indians got sick in the woods, you would die before they would. Indians have lived in Texas a lot longer than us. There is a tree that has leaves like the oak tree they roast, then boil, to give them energy.[1] They have a plant called 'snow on the prairie' that when you get all stopped up, will empty you quicker than you can get your britches off.[2]

When your head gets all clogged up with your nose running as you cough your lungs out, they recommend you swallow a red pepper no bigger than your smallest fingernail.[3] See that plant over there called the 'purple cornflower,' it grows all over Texas and they claim it cures everything."[4]

Suddenly shots rang out and Comanche ponies poured up the slope. The four of us had long discussed what to do in such a situation. We immediately dropped what we were doing and ran into my house which was a small rock fortress. Each of us climbed to our designated corner of the house. Climbing up to the wooden platforms, we grabbed the guns we had stored in our corners for such an event.

The first Comanche pass had roared through the Karankawa camp. One of the Karankawa lay on the ground a spear sticking out of his belly. A second Karankawa warrior was riddled with arrows. A third was firing arrows as even the squaws took up sticks to wave at the marauding Comanche. You could hear the raiders laugh as the squaw hit one of the Comanche not keeping a safe distance.

Two of the squaws had been below the dam with the children when the attack began. They wasted little time deliberating where to go as they began the seventy-five-yard sprint to our rock house. The sudden movement caught the Comanche's attention and seven of them peeled out after the group.

I called out to Dennis and Darryl who ran to my end of the building. The squaws and children were only forty yards from the building when it became apparent they would not make it. Just before the Comanche reached the children the four of us fired in unison. Four Comanche hit the ground, their heads, or chests, a mass of blood and gore.

The three remaining Comanche rode on through the small group. The lead Comanche speared a squaw, while another leaned down and grabbed the six-year-old Karankawa boy. The third warrior was shot off his horse by Kel who had immediately grabbed and fired a second rifle. When the remaining Comanche heeled his horse and turned, three rifle shots knocked him down.

Pulling the spear out of her companion, the uninjured squaw ran screaming down the slope toward the second group of Comanche. By the time her descent down the slope ended, her momentum had miraculously carried her into a Comanche that she speared like a pig.

The remaining Comanches laughed as the squaw pulled out the bloody spear and unsuccessfully slashed the air around them. They felt safe because of the distance from the house and just sat their horses watching the young woman waving her spear.

Kel, the best shot among us, grabbed his favorite Kentucky rifle and said, "Watch that young Chief." He pointed the rifle, took a long breath, and gently squeezed the trigger.

The rifle's loud crack and the Chief being blown off his horse happened in quick succession. Shrieking curses at the house, the surviving Comanches filled the young Karankawa squaw with arrows and rode off.

Returning to our four corners we surveyed the landscape. Six Comanche and one Karankawa lay between us and the dam. Down the slope, all the Karankawa looked dead, along with two Comanche. Eight dead Comanche, not bad.

Suddenly a wail rent the air, one of the children was still alive. I vaulted down the ladder and ran outside. The three-year-old Karankawa girl was clutching her bloody and very dead mother.

NOTES

1. Matt Turner, *Remarkable Plants of Texas* (Austin: University of Texas Press, 2009), 134-138.
2. Charles Hart, Tam Garland, Catherine Barr, Bruce Carpenter, and John Reagor, *Toxic Plants of Texas: Integrated Management Services to Prevent Livestock Losses* (Texas AgriLife Extension Service, 2003).
3. Turner, *Remarkable Plants of Texas*, 191-194.
4. Turner, *Remarkable Plants of Texas*, 210-213.

CHAPTER FIFTEEN

Kel and Darryl remained at their posts while Dennis and I made sure the remaining Comanche were not pretending to be dead. Once satisfied the Comanche posed no danger, I turned to the three-year-old Karankawa girl hugging her bloody mother. Kneeling, I gently picked the child up. Her eyes went wide as she struggled wildly to escape my arms. I spoke in a whisper and began to sing softly. The dark-haired child stopped struggling and warily watched my face as though trying to discern my intent. With a deep sigh, she just collapsed against my shoulder.

Kel and Darryl exited the house as Dennis yelled at them, "Dead Indians, just the way I like them."

Darryl responded, "Well happy boy, let's grab those Comanche ponies, looks like we just expanded our herd by eight horses." Grabbing ropes, we were able to lasso four of the ponies, but the others were half-wild and quickly scattered.

We drove the four horses into the corral and grabbed saddles for our mounts. The loose Comanche ponies offered a chase, but soon we had the remaining four in the corral. Like people, most horses preferred to be together rather than on their own.

"What should we do with these ponies?" inquired Dennis. "These eight, Rye's three, the two mules, and our three horses total sixteen animals. Taking care of that many animals is a lot of work."

"Several look like they were saddle stock at one time, I recommend we keep them. We may be able to trade or sell the others when we go to town," I offered.

"What about the kid?" asked Darryl.

Looking at the small bundle nestled against my shoulder, I softly said, "I don't know."

Gazing at the dead bodies between the house and the dam, and those down the hill, I said, "We need to bury these folks."

"The Indians?" sneered Dennis.

"Yes, the Indians. Do you want to smell rotten bodies for the next month?" I said with irritation.

"Shit," snarled Dennis. "Do what you want."

Kel spoke up, "I'll help you Rye." Dropping his voice to where Dennis could not hear, Kel said, "Rye, I would not be opposed to following your lead and treating the Indian dead with respect. We can bury the Karankawa and Comanche on the hill where you buried the previous four Comanche. The Comanche like to bury their dead facing east with their weapons.[1] I suspect we should do the same with the Karankawa, especially that squaw that fought so well."

Darryl said, "I will hitch up the mules to the wagon and haul the bodies up the hill if you boys will dig the graves."

Turning to Dennis, Darryl growled, "Get your ass into the wagon. You are going to help me pick up those bodies." Dennis started to refuse, but the glare from the normally placid Darryl stopped him before a word could form.

To Dennis's disgust, we dug sixteen graves, eight Karankawa and eight Comanche. Dennis argued the Comanche should be dumped in a single hole, but no one listened to him.

Before we placed the bodies in the graves, Kel suggested, "We should take any beadwork, arm bracelets, and weapons, and put them on top of each grave so that people know which Indian is which."

"What fucking bullshit," growled Dennis.

Without any rancor, Kel reasonably said, "Someday it might be important to this little girl to know which is her mama, and which one might be her dad or brother."

Dennis scowled, "So why are we going to bury the Comanche scum that killed her mama?"

Kel shook his head, "Don't know why. I just know it's right." Without saying a word, Kel began to remove the identifying articles from the bodies and set them aside. The bodies were placed in the graves, dirt shoveled in to form a small mound, and rocks laid over the fresh dirt to keep the animals out. On top of the graves, the arm bands, beads, and weapons were placed with rocks anchoring them in place to keep the wind from blowing them away.

The last to be buried was the brave young Karankawa woman. On her grave we erected a board etched Brave Woman, June 14, 1840. By the time her grave was finished, the light was beginning to fade. When we woke up this morning no one had anticipated spending the day digging graves.

• • •

When the sun set it was difficult to separate from little Kara. That was the name we gave her. No one knew her Indian name. She was a Karankawa, and we just shortened it to Kara. The name was short, and everyone could say it.

Kara was as wary as a packrat. She had big brown eyes that seemed almost as big as her head. The way that child would stare at your face was unnerving. It was as though she was working hard to decipher our thoughts and intentions.

We were cowboys and did not know much about kids, but we knew Kara was tiny for a three-year-old. The Karankawa had been eating poorly for a long time and Kara was as small as a large doll.

To everyone's relief, I pointed out my observation that it was like we had a doll in the house. All of us had sisters who we observed taking care of dolls. We watched our sisters dress, bathe, and feed their dolls. Each of us figured we could take care of a doll and proceeded to do so.

Though he hated Indians, Dennis was the best with a needle and thread among the four of us. He took remnants from a deer hide Kel had worked into soft leather. Dennis sewed together little leggings and a top for Kara. We hunted up different plants, roots, and flowers to grind into colors, then we all took turns painting little figures on the clothes.

Kel went hunting and returned with a fat doe. We were all excited at the prospect of making some moccasins, a hat, and a nightgown for little Kara. Grown men playing with a doll, who would have thought?

At night Kara would only sleep with me. The first night we kept trying to get her to sleep on the floor by the fire. Within a minute of putting Kara down, we would catch her trying to climb the ladder to where I slept. Out of fear Kara would fall and break a leg or arm, I relented and carried her up the ladder. When I put Kara down in my little sleeping corner, she quickly snuggled in my arms and was immediately asleep.

Kit did not mind sharing my bed with Kara. Nor was Kara afraid of Kit. Having two little bodies pressed against mine was a strange sensation. Knowing they found reassurance in my presence was completely unexpected. What a far cry this was from the horrors of war.

NOTES

1. Marvin Hunter, *The Boy Captives* (San Angelo, TX: Anchor Publishing Co., 1927, 1995), 132. The citation above refers to the seventh reprint in 1995.

CHAPTER SIXTEEN

The next morning, with little Kara sitting in my lap, and a five-month-old Kit sprawled across her lap, we discussed our next task, the creation of a decoy mine. We wanted protection in case the Republic of Texas, General Land Office, or some crooked politician decided to steal our land by saying the survey was wrong. Crossing off several locations, we picked a site down the hill far enough away that it was off my homestead, but close enough we could see if anyone was trespassing at the fake mine.

In case people wondered why we did not build our house next to the mine, we would tell them we did not want to hear the noise of mining in the house. If pressed why we did not include the mine on the one-hundred-acre homestead, we would say the need had not occurred to us. Being simple cowboys, it was easy to be underestimated.

Gathering up our picks and shovels, we hunted for a spot that offered a mixture of rock and dirt that could be quickly molded into a mine. We picked a likely spot where there was a rock seam bordered by dirt. Fortunately, the dead miner had left behind several small kegs of black powder. Hauling that explosive material must have been a hair-raising experience for the old miner.

Since none of us had ever worked with explosives, we used small amounts the first week. We blew holes just big enough to scare but not kill us. Using the rock hauler and long ropes, the mules hauled the debris out of the expanding tunnel, and we dropped the tailings down the slope.

Our luck held up, as our plan worked in placing the mine at the point where the dirt stopped, and a seam of rock started. We did not have to blast much to create one cave wall of rock while we shored up the opposite earthen wall with timber. Having a big slag pile for people to see how much work had been done to the mine was important, so we blasted extra rock just for appearance's sake. Absent a slag pile, people would be very suspicious about whether the mine was the source of the gold.

In the evening we would gather at the decoy mine to admire the day's handiwork. We could see how one might derive satisfaction from being a miner. Every day the hole in the hill got bigger as the pile outside grew larger. You could see the visible fruits of your labor.

To our pleasure, each evening as the sun began its descent, dots of light appeared as fireflies rose out of the meadow. Their lights pulsating as though the earth was breathing.

Dennis and Darryl argued endlessly about whether the insects were fireflies or lightning bugs. They continuously tried to rope others in to support their positions, but we all declined to choose a side.

The wetter it got, the more numerous the fireflies seemed to get. We had four inches of rain in June, and July seemed to be on tap for the same. With the increased rain, we realized how lucky we were to build our two homes on a slope not directly downstream from the canyon. When it rained, all the water was channeled into the canyon and the dry stream bed became a raging torrent that ripped apart anything in its path.

After an especially hard rain, Kel excitedly returned from a hunting trip to insist we follow him several miles south. Practically dancing with glee, Kel said, "With all the dirt and debris washed away, as clear as day you can see wagon ruts worn into the limestone stream bed."

We mounted up and five miles south the wagon ruts were unmistakable. Growing up in Texas, we had heard rumors the Spanish used the San Saba River as a road whenever it was dry, but no one believed the rumors.[1] Pointing at the tracks, I grinned and said, "It's true."

• • •

Working in the mine during the summer months was lucky timing. Outside, the fierce sun burnt one's skin and you felt like you were living in an oven. Each foot tunneled deeper into the hillside the temperature in the cool dark earth dropped, allowing us to dig in comfort. Instead of dreading the mine work, we counted ourselves lucky to be inside and not outside hauling rock.

At the end of three months, we had the rough makings of a mine six feet tall, three-foot-wide, and forty feet deep into the hillside angling away from our homestead. We shored up the ceiling with timber and built a massive oak door at the mine entrance. The door was secured by a thick chain and a cast-iron lock. The enormous lock looked impressive, but it would not stop anyone for very long.

Kel leaned against the massive mine door and smiled. "I recommend we take several of the gold bags and salt the mine. If somehow someone gets into the mine, we need them to believe it's the genuine article."

We all agreed. Hoofing it up the hill, I returned with three bags of gold-veined quartz. To Kara's delight, we let her sprinkle the gold-laden crystal throughout the mine's floor. Even in the dim torchlight, the floor glistened impressively. Kara stared contentedly at the glistening mine. Staring at the crystal and gold particles shining in our hands, Kara leaned toward me and whispered, "Fairy dust."

When we put Kara to bed at night we all took turns telling her stories. Several of Kara's favorites were the ones Dennis recited about Irish fairies. That is why when Kara saw the mine floor glistening, she thought it was fairy dust.

Even though Dennis continued to proclaim his hatred of Indians, he was finding it hard to feel any hostility toward Kara. Dennis was fortunate he did not display any hostility toward Kara, the rest of us would have beaten the hostility out of him.

Dennis loved to tell stories. We three grown men had heard his stories before and would groan when he started to tell them, again. Unlike her fathers, Kara was content to have the same story told four or five times in a sitting. That arrangement pleased Dennis and Kara both to no end.

Sitting around the cave's entrance we discussed our next step. We could pretend to continue working the mine, but none of us had the heart to waste time in a fake mine. Since it was supposed to be a working mine, we were bound to slip up with how much work was being done, or how much ore was being processed. Besides, if someone spent enough time in the mine, they were bound to suspect it was a decoy. We needed a way to explain why we were no longer working the mine.

Darryl smiled and suggested, "We can tell people the mine ran dry and collapsed. Let's mine another twenty feet and blow up the end."

Very carefully we loaded the end of the mine with a larger than usual load of powder and lit the fuse. With a thunderous explosion, the end of the tunnel collapsed. The result was convincing. The last ten feet was a huge pile of rock mixed with broken timbers where the ceiling and walls had collapsed.

We felt pretty satisfied until Kel said, "Trouble is that none of the rock in the slag pile has any crystal in it, yet all our gold comes from the gold veined crystal. I hate to say it, but we need to work in the real mine separating gold from the crystal. Then we need to dump the crystal on the fake mine's slag pile."

No one was happy with the prospect of more mine work, but we all saw the wisdom in Kel's comments. Dennis came up with a great suggestion. "Let's transfer all those rattlesnakes to the decoy mine. Take that big rattlesnake skin and nail it to the mine door with a warning that hundreds of rattlers are inside. We can tell people there was a cave-in and a crevice opened up containing hundreds of huge rattlers. Rather than risk our lives in a cave with no more gold, we decided to invest in cattle ranching."

Everyone agreed that was a great idea, but how to catch and move the rattlers? Kel shared, "I have seen Indians take a ten-foot leather rope with a loop at the end attached to an equally long stick. You drop the loop around the snake's head and tighten it. The loop holds the snake ten feet away, so it cannot bite you. We can build a big wooden barrel to drop the snakes into, haul the barrel down to the mine, and set it rolling to the back of the mine where it will tip over and release the snakes."

Kel looked at everyone expecting a hearty endorsement of his idea. Instead, everyone looked at him in horror.

"What?" a puzzled Kel asked.

Over the next two hours, a variety of alternatives was discussed. To everyone's dismay, Kel's suggestion was the best. Finally, people discussed which jobs they were most comfortable with, and all agreed Kel would be the snake wrangler. I would open and close the barrel as each new rattlesnake was inserted. Dennis would hold two torches to provide light for both catching and releasing the snakes. Darryl held a shotgun he would use if any snakes got loose or decided to charge us.

The shaky plan came apart from the start. Kel had a hard time separating one rattlesnake from the others. Once he finally did, Kel stood so far back from the barrel that he could not see the barrel rim very well. When Kel loosened the leather loop, the rattlesnake dropped on the outside of the barrel next to where I was standing. Darryl shot at the snake, missed, and blew a huge hole in the side of the barrel. I danced away from the dual threat of the snake and Darryl's shotgun.

A quick retreat up the ladders to the sunlight was followed by an hour of yelling and finger-pointing. Eventually, we agreed a ramp would be built that Kel would walk up so that he was up and above the barrel mouth with the stick deep in the barrel when the snake was released.

We returned to the cave with a new tall thin barrel, built a ramp, and agreed to test the new system out with a small snake. The system worked. During six nerve-racking hours, averaging fifteen snakes an hour, we barreled up close to a hundred rattlers that were not happy at being dropped into a wooden container.

Most accidents happen just as quitting time approaches. Kel dropped the last snake in, was not watching his feet, and fell off the ramp. His full weight fell against the side of the barrel and in slow motion, the barrel began to wobble.

With horror, I watched as the barrel began to tip toward me. I froze as my mind raced with the alternatives, run, or throw my weight against the barrel in the hope of rebalancing the snake-filled barrel. If successful, the barrel would roll back into position. If unsuccessful, the barrel would roll over on me as a hundred angry snakes poured out.

In my mind, I was running with a hundred snakes chasing me. In reality, my body slammed against the barrel stopping its disastrous tilt.

Everyone froze as a collective moan of relief echoed off the cave walls. With trembling hands, we nailed the barrel top on, and with three times as many ropes as necessary, hauled the barrel from the cave floor up through the two-foot-wide slit and onto a waiting wagon. Securing the barrel in the wagon with multiple ropes, we cautiously went down the hill to the decoy mine.

Gingerly lowering the barrel to the ground. We removed all but one of the nails keeping the lid on the barrel. The remaining nail barely held the lid. With dread, we lowered the barrel to its side. With a mighty push, we shoved the barrel into the mine where it crashed. The lid flew off and a hundred pissed-off rattlers poured out of that barrel looking for something to bite. We slammed the mine door and shivered with nervous relief. Each of us checked to make sure we had not wet ourselves.

The following day we carefully descended into the real mine. Building a huge fire that lit up the cave, we searched for any snakes we might have missed. Seeing none, we cautiously began to peel the crystal off the walls, glancing left and right the entire time. We were lucky the crystal just crumbled off the wall.

After hauling the raw material up, we set up stumps near the decoy mine where we gently hammered the crystal and separated the gold. Though we were careful, our hands were a chewed-up mess from crystal cuts. We spent a month throwing the crystal onto the slag pile until we felt no one could question whether it was the real source of our gold. To our good fortune, we also ended up with twenty bags of roughly processed gold.

NOTES

1. Greg Walton, *Bear Meat 'n' Honey* (Austin, TX: Acorn Press, 1990), 69. In *Bear Meat 'n' Honey* this story is shared by Roy LaFayette Walton who was born in 1903 five miles south of Lost Maples. The story was originally told to Roy by Hiram Thompson whose family was one of the earliest in the San Sabinal Canyon. People report that even today the wagon ruts are visible in the limestone stream bed.

CHAPTER SEVENTEEN

Kel, Darryl, and Dennis were giddy with excitement when I encouraged them to pick out their five thousand acres. I pointed out the boundaries on my one-hundred-acre homestead and the surrounding five thousand acres. Their excitement faltered when I pointed out we needed to mark their boundaries with rocks.

Fortunately, with the arrival of September, fall was in the air. Summer's oppressive heat and heavy air were gone. Days were not yet marked by coolness, but by a refreshing absence of heat. The weather had reached that magical time between seasons when the earth and its inhabitants let out a sigh of relief.

We spent the week scouting our one hundred and twenty thousand acres.[1] With anticipation we explored our canyon and the two adjacent canyons. The four of us walked the canyon bottoms checking for springs, potential lumber, fruit trees, and trails. We climbed the canyon walls and walked along the flat mountain tops identifying pastures while looking at the canyon floor two thousand feet below us.

Each of us commented appreciably about the wildness of the canyons and the beauty of the steep landscape. We recognized the need to surround the mine with all the canyon acreage we could muster, but at the same time, we looked longingly south. From the canyon tops, we could see how once you got out of our narrow canyon, further south the steep canyon walls gradually spread out from one another. Five miles south of the canyon mouth, was a beautiful valley several miles wide stretching off in the distance as far as you could see.

Kel said, "On the ride here we went to San Antonio and then directly west until we met the Sabinal River. We followed the river north until we came to your canyon. I gotta tell you, beautiful country lays to the south. The Sabinal River is clear as day and bordered by the loveliest cypress trees I think I have ever seen. Pecan trees were so thick in some areas that I bet you have to wade through the pecans in November."

I was enthralled by their description. "Tell you what. Let's build our canyon boundaries now. When we go to Austin, we will also lay claim to some of that quality pastureland we can see from the canyon top."

Kel, Dennis, and Darryl stopped looking south. Everyone's preference for land was different. In the end, each person was delighted with their homestead and the five thousand surrounding acres.

Darryl's homestead was a meadow of little bluestem grass atop a flat mountain top. Dennis' homestead contained a large spring, and his five thousand acres included a trickle of water and several clear pools of spring-fed water. Kel picked the wildest section, just a jumble of rocks, trees, and steep slopes.

Starting with my homestead's hundred acres, we dropped a rock every three steps around the entire section. We did the same for the one hundred-acre homesteads for Dennis, Kel, and Darryl. Though not walled, from a distance our homestead boundaries were visible as dotted lines of rock.

Next, we stacked rock three high every one hundred yards around my entire five thousand acres, creating an even larger buffer around the mine. Fortunately, there was rock everywhere and one did not have to travel far to find material. While the boundary was sporadic now, a time would come when we would build entire walls as a boundary to help clear the fields of rock. Someday we would want to convert the land to pasture and raise crops.

When my land was marked, we started on five thousand-acre boundaries for Kel, Dennis, and Darryl. By the end of this three-week process, we were jerking in our beds as we stacked rock in our sleep.

The task was daunting to think of stacking rock around our one hundred and twenty thousand-acre holdings, but we knew we must. At Darryl's suggestion, we took a week's break from stacking rock and just relaxed. We fished, hunted, and played games with Kara. Kel took her into the woods and taught Kara how to track animals and hunt. Dennis showed her how to sew. Me, I was just the person she turned to when excited or scared.

During our week break, birds began their migration south. The boys were amazed by the size of the hawk kettles flying overhead. Kel and Dennis were overjoyed when several days later geese and ducks began filling the sky by the thousands and then tens of thousands. Thanks to Kel, we had goose or duck every night for a month.

Just when the boys thought they could not be surprised, thousands of butterflies appeared on their journey south. So many butterflies perched on tree limbs, that the limbs groaned under the weight.

While the migrations were still occurring, our week of rest ended, and we went back to working on the outer boundary for our one hundred and twenty thousand acres. We cut stakes two-foot-long and carved the date and our names on one side. On the other side, we carved the words "boundary stake." We buried the stakes below the surface of the ground at the corner of each property. If our rocks were ever illegally moved, we would unbury the stakes in front of the law.

The first week of November, we began the soul-numbing task of building stone cairns three rocks high every hundred yards around our one hundred and twenty thousand acres. Fortunately, we were distracted by the maple trees exploding into color. Splashes of orange, yellow, and glorious red surrounded us each day as we stacked rock.

Consulting Professor Eldridge's book, I was able to tell the others we had bigtooth, red, and yellow maples in the canyons. According to the book, none produced the sap required for maple syrup. Though we delighted in the maples, we were alarmed to read if horses ate the dried maple leaves, the leaves could kill them. We would have to fence off the canyon mouth to keep the horses out.

While working on the fence we saw a variety of wildlife. By standing still and avoiding noise, it was not uncommon to see six-month-old bobcats trailing after their mothers through tumbled boulders. Once a porcupine family lumbered by grunting and groaning with each step. Flocks of turkeys scampered through the underbrush and roosted in tall pecan trees at night.

Packs of javelinas were everywhere. We had to keep them out of our pasture and the dammed water. The javelinas shit and pissed everywhere, fouling the water something fearsome. Kel picked off the javelina in the daytime, while Kit stalked the javelina at night. Though Kel was a good shot, Kit's taste for javelina convinced the survivors to water elsewhere.

The last week of November, after three months of fighting rock, cactus, snakes, bugs, and the sun, we decided it was time to surrender and just call it "good enough." We retired to the cabin and began to heal our cuts, bruises, and sore muscles.

That first night after finishing, or more accurately, abandoning the boundary marking, we felt satisfied. We had constructed a water system to the house, built a dam that provided water for irrigation, erected a second bigger house, carved a decoy mine out of the hill, and placed an incomplete but visible stone boundary around our land.

Sitting in front of a campfire burning down to glowing coals, I said, "Boys, now comes the tricky part. We cannot waltz into town with a bunch of Spanish gold bars. The Republic might try to claim it is Mexican war spoils and try to confiscate it."

"I recommend we use our ax to chop each gold bar into two-inch slices and then cut those slices into four pieces. We can melt the pieces in the cast-iron pots and pour the metal into the molds I bought. Plus, that old miner had two molds for what looks like small cannonballs. Chopping and melting will be a time-consuming process, but the balls will make it look like we refined the gold ourselves."

Dennis said, "Before we spend weeks melting gold, let's go pick up as many pecans as we can before those wild javelinas eat them all."

The next day felt like a picnic as we rode five miles south to a huge stand of pecan trees. We loaded sacks, boxes, and then wagons full of pecans.[2] After two days, even Dennis realized we could spend a month picking up pecans and there would still be more on the ground. We called the pecan picking quits and shifted to melting gold.

For two weeks we chopped, melted, and molded gold. Melting gold was a dangerous job. If any of that liquid gold touched our fingers or toes, the hot metal would have burned them right off. We worked in pairs for an hour at a time. Fatigue increased the chances of causing a permanent injury. If anyone witnessed a lack of concentration on the part of someone, they called an immediate halt and we stopped. All the gold in the world was not worth an arm or a leg.

On December 13, after two tense weeks, we guessed we had two thousand pounds of gold. Staring at the bags of gold, we found it hard to believe it belonged to us. We agreed when we deposited the gold, each of us would carry a bag of gold quartz. If challenged by someone to prove how we obtained the gold, we would show them the gold-veined quartz.

That night, as we sipped warm bear broth in the crisp December air, I turned to Dennis and thanked him for the soup and all the other meals he provided. Soon everyone joined in to thank him.

Since his arrival in April, Dennis had been cooking for us. Dennis was the acknowledged expert at roasting everything that roamed the canyon on four legs such as deer, bear, rabbit, and even the greasy javelina. He was an expert at preparing winged creatures that lived in the canyon such as turkey and dove, as well as fowl like the geese and ducks that migrated through our area in the spring and fall.

The mastery of cooking meat was not enough for Dennis. He possessed the knowledge to harvest everything in the woods as well because you never knew when game would be scarce. From buffalo gourds the size of your fist, Dennis would roast the seeds and spread them on a dish. Dennis cooked some greens he called goosefoot that smelled like dirty socks but tasted good. He constantly harangued us to keep our eyes open for wild onions he used to flavor half our meals. Though the name pigweed was not attractive, when boiled, the plant accompanied many a meal since pigweed grew year-round.

One time I remarked on having seen some cattails and Dennis made me go back and harvest them. Dennis explained that we could eat the young tubers. If caught before they ripened, we could roast the brown cattail tops.

Dennis was also one hell of a baker. In early May he made cobbler out of the last blackberries of the season. He made jam out of the mustang grapes, or muscadines as some people called them, that grew in long vines on the forest edge. Searching the woods throughout the year he made jam from peaches, persimmons, plums, and cherries. From spring until fall, different types of cactus produced fruit as sweet and tasty as candy. When we harvested pecans in November, Dennis made pecan pie.

I carried the professor's book with me everywhere and added notes about the things Dennis fed us. True to my vow, I was going to help Zeke add to his book. The book already had chapters on trees, plants, foods, poisons, medicine, and what Zeke called mind changers, things if you ate them you had visions.

Mind changers were already familiar to me. Agave was a kind of cactus the Mexicans and Indians harvested for a strong kind of drink that made the world spin. Drinking fermented wild mustang grapes could lead to the feeling you had too much whiskey. Peyote cactus harvested from the banks of the Rio Grande River was used by natives for visions and valued as trade items. Me, I did not want to take or drink anything that would impact my ability to protect myself.

NOTES

1. Those of you familiar with the Lost Maples State Natural Area in Texas may recognize the boundaries of the ranch and the park are almost the same. You may realize the ranch's eastern boundary encompasses the 3.1-mile East Trail (which includes the .8-mile Maple Trail). The East Trail follows the Sabinal River north, turns left to follow Hollow Creek, and then southeast, as it follows Can Creek back to the starting point where the Sabinal River and Can Creek meet. The western border of the ranch is similar to the 3.6-mile Lost Maples West Trail. The West Trail follows Can Creek northwest, south through Mystic Canyon, and east back to the starting point on Can Creek.

2. Walton, *Bear Meat 'n' Honey*, 178. This story was shared in *Bear Meat 'n' Honey* by Hub Thompson who was born on the Sabinal River in Bandera County, Texas in 1901. The story was shared with Hub by his grandfather Gideon Thompson whose family settled in the San Sabinal Canyon in 1852. Grandpa Gideon told Hub there were so many pecans they would load them in wagons and take them to San Antonio to trade for groceries.

CHAPTER EIGHTEEN

The following morning, the fourteenth of December, with the sun barely revealing a faint yellow glow to the east, I walked out the front door and to my astonishment, dozens of Comanche were stealing our horses. I jerked the Colt Paterson out of my holster and fired in rapid succession dropping four Comanche as the rest abandoned the horses and fled. Darryl burst out the door behind me yelling at the top of his voice. Rifles poked out the second level of the house as Kel and Dennis fired at the departing Comanche knocking down another two.

Kel who had the best eyesight erupted out of the house with two rifles and three pistols strapped every which way across his body. Without pausing, Kel yelled, "Rye, grab your weapons and saddle up three horses while I do the same."

I just stood there frozen. "Why?"

With a forlorn look, Kel said, "They have Kara."

Kel's words galvanized me into action. Questions about how Kara ended up outside went unasked. I rushed into the house for my rifles, water, and a pack of food.

Dennis and Darryl started saddling up the horses. "We are going too."

With a murderous glare Kel said, "No, Rye and I will each take three of our best horses. Those Comanche will run their horses to death. We will never catch them with one horse each. The only hope is if Rye and I swap horses till the Comanche horses start to die."

"We will follow them for a day. Rye will stop with three horses and wait until I return. I suspect I will catch up with them on the second or third day. By the time I get back to Rye, my three horses will be done. Rye, I need you to keep your horses saddled and fresh."

"Dennis, you wanted to kill Indians, here is your chance. After we leave, you and Darryl pick out the best six horses left. We will not be trying to hide our tracks, so you should be able to easily follow. Walk your horses, do not tire them. When you see us running, I want you and Dennis ready to ambush the Comanche. I fear that war party may follow us back to Lost Maples. We need to be ready for a running battle all the way home."

Without another word, Kel jumped on his horse and with the other two horses trailing behind, he took off after the Comanche. Several minutes later, I was in the saddle and chasing Kel's dust. We rode at a rapid pace that was cruel to the horses. When one horse tired we simply slid up next to a fresh horse and leaped from one saddle to the next, our feet never touching the ground.

Being the best woodsman among us, Kel had no trouble following the Comanche despite their many efforts to throw us off their trail. Kel followed them unwaveringly as though he was traveling in the group ahead. We rode through the morning, afternoon, evening, and even into the night.

The full moon, what some call a Comanche moon, was so bright visibility was as good as when dawn first breaks. Without the full moon, we would never have been able to trail the Comanche at night.

When the sun rose across the horizon Kel stopped. We had been riding for an entire day and night. Examining all six horses, Kel picked the three that appeared to have been least damaged by the punishing ride.

Grimly Kel said, "I figure to ride hard and catch them by nightfall. You ride along slowly behind me, stop if you lose my trail. Do not tire your horses. Stop at midday and spend the night. After I grab Kara, I will kill these horses getting back to you."

I wanted to argue with Kel, but he was right. The Comanche might not see Kel. If they did, they would not be worried about a lone pursuer. That would be their mistake.

Slowly following the tracks of Kel's three horses, I followed him another six hours. With the sun high overhead, I unsaddled the horses, rubbed them down, watered, and staked them out to eat the buffalograss growing on the border of a small, wooded area. I figured to leave the horses unsaddled during the day and most of the night.

Every four hours I watered the horses, but not so much that they were full. I needed them ready to run, not hindered by thirst nor bloated with water bellies. Despite my lack of appetite, I forced myself to eat some jerky. I wished I was the one saving Kara, but Kel was the right person.

Against my will, a nagging worry began to gnaw at me. What would I do if Kel did not return tomorrow? Should I wait another day or go in search of him? A series of potential calamities raced through my mind. To combat the uneasiness building in me, I took out my Patersons and began to clean them, one gun at a time. After cleaning the two pistols, I took out my Kentucky long rifles and cleaned them. When I finished cleaning the last rifle, my mind felt ordered and disciplined.

My thoughts turned to actions I needed to take when Kel returned. Before bed, I would water each horse and stake them out close to me but where they could eat during the night. I would wake up before dawn, saddle the horses, and hold the reins for a quick departure. When Kel arrived, Kara and I would mount one horse and Kel a second. We would take the third horse and any others that were not ruined yet as we raced home. I refitted my guns so that I could hold Kara with my left arm while I fired from my right over my left shoulder.

Before the sun rose, I was standing with the reins for the three horses tightly gripped in my left hand with my right hovering over my pistol. A slow hour passed, then an even slower second hour. By the end of the third hour, my rigid posture was causing pain and the horses were restless.

I fought back my rising panic by putting my previous plan into action. I allowed the horses a small drink each and then stood with them in the grass, so they could graze while we waited.

The sun rose directly overhead, and my eyes hurt from squinting at the distant horizon.

Suddenly, something on the horizon caught my attention. I focused so hard my head began to ache. A small dot appeared at the top of a ravine and then disappeared down its backside. Praying that I was not fooling myself by imagining it was Kel, I stared until my eyes watered and blurred. Shaking my head, I rubbed my eyes. Kel and Kara were coming. I jumped into the saddle and held the other two horses tightly.

Kel practically slammed his horse into mine and threw Kara into my arms. To my surprise, he unbuttoned my jacket and buttoned it again with Kara inside. Kel yelled, "We have some hard riding, that will keep her from falling." I held out the reins of the fresh grulla dun and Kel jumped from his faltering mount to the dun all in one quick motion. Reaching around, Kel pulled the reins of the seal skin bay whose chest was heaving but was struggling less than his other two worn-out mounts. Spurring our four horses, we fled across the land.

We ran the horses hard, switching rides before any horse completely played out. For three hours we ran the horses unmercifully, their coats glistening with sweat, and foam bubbling from their nostrils.

Dennis and Darryl were so well hidden we did not see them when we flew past. Suddenly behind us, there was a cavalcade of shots that sounded like a dozen rifles. Over our shoulders, we saw half a dozen Comanche tumble from their horses, as rifle and then pistol shots rang out.

The shocked Comanche scattered as Dennis and Darryl grabbed their mounts and thundered after us. When Dennis and Darryl reached us with their fresh mounts we switched horses. With six fresh horses among the four of us, we sped away, confident for the first time.

Seeing our escape, the scattered Comanche bunched up and began pursuing us. The war party had already lost some horses in the pursuit, but the Comanche's exhausted ponies hit the limits of their endurance all at once, stumbling and dying by the handfuls.

We dropped into a small gulley and I said, "No more running. Hide the horses, we are going to kill these Comanche."

When the Comanche rounded the rock twenty feet away they met a wall of gunfire. Shooting as fast as we could work our pistols and rifles we butchered the Indians. Silence settled in as the echoes of our shots began to fade.

Turning to Darryl, Dennis said, "Take Kara home. There are Comanche afoot for twenty miles back. I am going to make sure they never return."

Kel said, "Even afoot those Comanche are dangerous. I'll go with you."

"Me too," I said. "We rode our horses hard, but if any survived, I want them back."

• • •

Kel, Dennis, and I spent the next four days trailing Comanche and catching worn-out horses. The war party had hit several homesteads before us and were taking captives back to their camp.

During those four days, we came across several dead or dying captives. One was a boy of seven or eight who either fell or was thrown off a horse. We found his body by the trail, his neck at an angle that showed he died when he hit the ground.

Another was a dying young woman who said her name was Sarah McCullough. She had tried to escape during the chase. One look and we could tell her back and right leg were broken. Struggling to speak through the pain, Sarah said, "The Comanche killed my husband during the raid on our farm." Then she began to wail pitifully, "Those demons took me and my baby during the raid. My baby, my baby, they killed my baby that first day because he was crying."

Sarah, though dying, clutched Dennis by the arm and begged him, "There are two more captives, a seven-year-old boy and a seventeen-year-old girl. You must save them."

We struggled with what to do with Sarah and the boy's bodies. Taking them home for a Christian burial was our first preference, but there might be a live seventeen-year-old that we needed to save.

Wrapping the two bodies tightly in blankets, we buried them after a quick service. If we found the girl quick enough, we would dig up the bodies and take them home.

The very next Comanche we came upon was sprawled out next to a dead horse. Dennis went to get off his horse and the Comanche rolled over and fired an arrow that went through the meaty part of Dennis's upper arm. A .62 caliber slug from Kel's Baker rifle slammed the Comanche backward into the hard ground.

Fortunately for Dennis, the arrow had a small flint head, the kind typically used for hunting birds. The point went completely through Dennis's arm without producing a lot of blood. We broke off the arrow and pulled it through. A little whiskey, a clean bandage, a lot of complaining from Dennis, and his arm was usable. From then on, every time we approached a supposedly dead Comanche, we put a bullet through their head from a safe distance.

Most of the live Comanche we encountered were by themselves or at the most, in pairs. Half the time when we rode up, the Comanche were busy cooking the horse they rode to death. The other half of the time the lone or paired Comanche tried to ambush us.

After several fights, it dawned on us none of the Comanche had ammunition for their guns and few had arrows. They had used most of their gunpowder and arrows raiding other farms.

When the Comanche hit Lost Maples, they made the mistake of trying to make one last raid when they were low on ammunition and arrows. That explained why the Comanche who outnumbered us ten to one, were quick to flee when they encountered gunfire during the attempt to steal our horses.

Tomahawks and knives were no match for guns. I guess you could call it a massacre, something you do not repeat with pride around a campfire. But they had stolen Kara, killed Sarah's husband and baby, as well causing the death of that little boy, Sarah, and maybe the girl. Without any hesitation, we killed every remaining Comanche where they stood.

We came across a situation that got us scratching our heads. The Comanche with the scarred forehead that attacked the ranch back in February, lay sprawled out on the ground next to a dead horse. A large stone lay inside the Comanche's crushed skull. Studying the signs, Kel determined the horse died while running and the Comanche was thrown in the air. The warrior must have been stunned or knocked out when he hit the ground. Someone took a stone and smashed in his skull as he lay on the ground.

Circling wide of the dead horse, Kel started to chuckle. "I think we found the girl. Looks like they were riding double, and both got thrown when the horse died. While he lay on the ground she caved in his skull. Smart girl, she took a piece of brush and wiped out her tracks. There is a small heel print going in that direction. This girl has spunk."

With Kel leading, we followed the scant trail left by the girl. After a hundred yards, Kel pointed to a small brushy knoll and called out softly, "Girl, we mean you no harm. We killed those Comanche."

There was no response. Dennis holstered his pistol and walked forward with his hands in the air. He stopped and stood very still. With firmness, Dennis said, "You are safe now." Walking forward three more steps, to our amazement, Dennis took off his jacket and laid it across the backside of the bush. We heard a whimper of pain.

From behind the bush stepped out a naked young woman who winched as she walked. The whimper we heard was not from fear, but from the pain where Dennis's jacket touched her body. Her pale skin had been roasted by the sun. The skin on her face, neck, shoulders, arms, legs, breasts, and back had burned, peeled, and then burned again.

Glancing at the crisp skin, Kel said, "We have to find this girl some water and shade." Turning to the young woman Kel gently said, "Getting on a horse is going to hurt, but we must find shade and water to bathe your skin. I know it is uncomfortable to be naked with us, but you cannot drape Dennis's jacket over your shoulders, it will rub you raw and hurt more."

Grimacing, Dennis gently removed the jacket and helped the young woman climb onto a horse. She held the reins with blistered hands and though tears of pain ran down her cheeks, the young woman did not utter a sound.

Returning to a spot we passed a mile earlier, we pulled into a small canyon drenched in cool shade. Kel nodded toward a stopping point on the creek containing a deep spring.

Dennis helped the young woman off the horse as she barely stifled a moan. Her jagged pain-filled gasps felt like a knife cutting through us all.

Kel pointed to the three-foot-deep pool of clear water. "Miss, you need to soak in that spring. The cool water will help with the pain and clean out the burns. While you are in there, I will hunt up some plants I need for a salve. Since the burns cover your whole body, we will lay out a blanket and cover it with the poultice you need for healing. You can lay face up or down on the blanket. We will then cover the other side of your body with the remaining poultice. There is no way to avoid you remaining naked, we are trying to save your life."

While she soaked in the pool, Kel searched the canyon. He came back with cactus, horsemint, huisache leaves, bark from the dogwood, and madrone leaves. Kel smashed them all up and made a gooey layer on the blanket. At Kel's direction, the young woman laid on the goo face up.

With a red face, Kel said, "I apologize, but someone has to rub this poultice all over your body."

She nodded her understanding. With resignation, she pointed at Dennis. His face flaming in embarrassment, Dennis winced as he applied the poultice to her face, neck, shoulders, arms, breasts, belly, legs, and feet. The entire time her eyes followed Dennis who periodically gazed into her face requesting permission to continue.

Kel boiled a tea in which bits of flower and bark floated. Handing her the cup, Kel said, "This tea is a mixture of a flower called mountain pink and bark from the black willow. The bittersweet taste may be a little off-putting, but the mixture will help with your fever."

Though in a hurry to return, everyone knew we would have to remain in place until the young woman could travel. Every day Dennis remained in the camp, helping her climb into the pool to soak, and then reapplying the poultice Kel showed him how to make.

While Dennis nursed the young woman, Kel and I roamed up and down the Comanche escape route looking for horses. There was no way to know how many horses the Comanche started with, but by the dead horses on the trail, it was evident they rode at least three dozen to death. Only three Comanche horses appeared to survive the chase. There may have been more surviving Comanche ponies, but we did not find them.

We started Kara's rescue with twelve horses and half survived. Fortunately, Woe was in great shape to start with and survived without injury. Woe would just need some time to rest up.

Kel's grulla dun survived. The horse had a gray mouse-colored coat with a dark stripe that ran across its back from its dark mane to its dark tail. Likewise, the Appaloosa won by Darryl in a poker game ended the chase worn out, but uninjured.

The two outlaw horses, the chestnut mare with the light mane and tail as well the seventeen hands tall seal skin bay stallion survived. I was never one to wish ill on horses, but to my chagrin, Dennis's sorry-looking sorrel somehow survived the punishing ride.

Like myself, both Kel and Darryl took good care of their horses. When stressed the horses responded well without breaking down. We were all surprised at Dennis' sorrel, who more or less, took care of himself.

Each day we kept adding horses to those staked out at the camp in the cool canyon. We would roll into camp with a newly retrieved horse or game such as rabbit, turkey, squirrel, and an occasional deer.

In a heavily accented voice, the young woman revealed her name was Heidi. With fierce determination, Heidi said, "I lived on a farm with my German parents and two older brothers a week's ride east of Lost Maples. Our farm was the first homestead raided." Thrusting her chin forward, she defiantly held back tears as she said, "Everyone in my family was killed."

"The first night I attempted to escape and as punishment, they took all my clothes. My long hair protected my neck for a while, but my pale skin burned to a bright red the first day and blistered that night. Each day the red skin would rub or peel off, and the exposed pink skin would redden and blister. I remember little of the raids on the flight west as the constant pain made my mind fuzzy."

Heidi continued, "I think the Comanche attacked five homesteads before your ranch. Two of the homesteads put up fierce fights. There was a big argument about whether to try to steal your horses because they were out of gunpowder and almost out of arrows. Fortunately for you, half of the war party decided the raid was not worth it and went north."

Though Heidi could have used more time to heal, after a week we felt a pressing need to return to the ranch. We rode a day south and dug up the bodies of Sarah and the boy who Heidi had gotten to know. After retrieving their bodies, a melancholy weighed Heidi down. I worried she was mourning not only the deaths of Sarah and the boy but shaken by the awareness her own body could have easily been draped over one of the horses.

Each night we stopped next to clean water so that Heidi could bathe, and a new layer of the poultice could be applied by Dennis. After three nights, it was with relief we saw the outline of our home.

Kara ran out of the house and jumped into my arms before I was fully out of the saddle. She hugged me and cried. Kara went around and around hugging the men in her life.

Darryl strode out and yelled, "Goodness gracious, I have been worried about you boys. I expected you back ten days ago."

Suddenly Darryl fell silent, unsure of what to make of the red, but healing young woman, wearing a huge hat weaved out of plants and a blanket that loosely covered her nakedness. After a week without clothes around strangers, Heidi had lost all self-awareness of nakedness. She gingerly dismounted and stuck out her hand, "Guten tag, I am Heidi."

Darryl recovered quickly. With a grin, he said, "Howdy, I am Darryl. Nice to meet you." Acting as though her condition was perfectly normal, he said, "Come on in, let me show you around."

We were worried about how Heidi would treat Kara, who even the blindest person could see was an Indian. With a soft voice, I explained, "Kara's entire Karankawa family was killed by the Comanche six months ago. Now Kara is our daughter and the most precious thing in our lives."

Heidi who had been so stoic and tough the entire time we had known her, burst into tears. To Kara's confusion, Heidi hugged her and sobbed. There was no need to worry about Heidi resenting Kara.

When Kara's people died, we buried them on a small hill behind the house with their weapons and jewelry on the stone atop each grave. While we were gone, Darryl buried the six Comanche killed when Kara was kidnapped. Each warrior got his own grave with his weapons and adornments atop the grave, six new graves. We had quite a graveyard, with eight Karankawa and fourteen Comanche graves.

Several Comanche survived our running battle and word spread about the fierce warriors at Lost Maples. Our reputation as warriors and the respect we showed their dead stopped the Comanche raids. Every other month we would come out to find something new had been added to a warrior's grave. We never saw them, and the Comanche never bothered us again.

After everyone unpacked, Kel said, "We need to get that woman and boy in the ground." A quick explanation was given to Darryl and then we had a short service from the good book. We buried Sarah and the boy next to the Karankawa. Dennis chiseled Sarah's name on a piece of slate for her headstone. He chiseled "good boy" on the slate headstone of the young boy.

Up until that night, a lot had gone unsaid about Kara and Heidi's rescue. Taking turns, each of us shared what had happened since we had all been together.

Kel stared at the fire with Kara sleeping soundly in my lap. "Shortly after I left Rye, I came across a dead Comanche pony. While we had been alternating three horses, the raiding party had been alternating two and it was taking a toll. The Comanche thought they would raid our ranch and come away with more ponies. Rye's quick response and our rifles forced them to escape without fresh ponies."

"In the late afternoon, I came across a second dead pony. I decided to tie two of my horses off in a small bunch of oak trees and see if I could approach unobserved by avoiding kicking up dust. Shortly after the sun went down I saw their camp. The Comanche had killed one of the ponies and a haunch of it was roasting over a small fire."

"I waited all night for them to fall asleep. Finally, the last one fell asleep two or three hours before dawn. It took me an hour to slowly work my way to where Kara was tied. Thank goodness Kara and I had spent time in the woods where I taught her how to walk quietly and soundlessly."

Turning to Heidi, Kel said, "Sorry Miss, but I did not see you or any of the others in the camp."

Heidi nodded, "We were in a camp further down the trail."

Kel continued, "Kara opened her eyes and blinked. She understood what we needed to do. A tense hour passed as Kara and I silently worked our way out of the camp and returned to my horse. We rode the horse to the other two who thankfully had not been attacked by prairie wolves while I was gone."

"I buttoned Kara up in the front of my jacket to have my hands free to control the reins and so that I could shoot." Smiling at the brilliance of his good idea, Kel continued, "All buttoned up with just her eyes showing I did not have to worry about losing Kara during the ride."

"While transferring horses, I saw the dust cloud behind us, and we ran those horses as hard as I safely could. The Comanche were uninterested in the health of their horses. They figured by running their horses to death, someone was bound to catch us. Rye, I was happy to see you were ready to ride when we came upon you. That was one wild ride."

Sitting around the fire that night we decided to raise the best horses money could buy. You never knew when a good horse might save your life. We would use the gold to invest in horse flesh as well as cattle.

Though six of our original eight Comanche ponies were lost or died during the chase, we found three surviving Indian ponies on the trail, and we had gained six ponies when the Comanche had attacked the ranch and stolen Kara. In the end, we gained three horses.

The ranch now consisted of seventeen horses and two mules. There was Woe, the chestnut mare, the seal brown bay stallion, Dennis' sorrel, Kel's dun, Darryl's Appaloosa, and eleven Comanche ponies.

During the battle with the Comanche, we picked up four worn-out Brown Bess' we would use for parts or trade, two Baker rifles, and a Kentucky rifle. We also gathered up a dozen tomahawks, a dozen knives, a half-dozen bows, and a nice Bowie knife.

Staring at the fire with bedtime just around the corner, a kind of awkwardness that had been absent from our time on the trail began to emerge. Turning to Heidi I said, "There is a private bedroom in the smaller stone house you are welcome to make your own."

Blinking slowly, Heidi asked, "Does anyone else sleep in the little stone house?"

Afraid she would think we were suggesting something improper I quickly reassured her, "Absolutely not, you would be the only one in the house."

Heidi stared silently a moment and then asked, "Where does Kara sleep?"

With a little embarrassment I explained, "Kara and Kit, uh, Kit is our pet cougar, sleep in that elevated platform in the corner with me."

Nodding her head somberly, Heidi said, "I will never feel safe in a house by myself." Looking Dennis in the eye, she asked, "Which platform do you sleep on?"

Dennis pointed to the far corner. With a firmness that left no room for argument, Heidi declared, "Dennis and I will share that corner."

From that night on, Dennis told us Heidi always slept on the opposite side of his corner. According to him, Heidi never initiated any type of romantic contact, but she always slept with one of her feet touching him. Heidi needed to know someone was there protecting her.

CHAPTER NINETEEN

For days after the Comanche chase, everyone was protective of Kara and anxiously watched her every movement. Several attempts to find out how the Comanche captured Kara were halted because she interpreted our anxiety as anger, causing Kara to shut down. Eventually, we were able to gently coax Kara into telling us she had gone outside to catch a fairy. Dennis had told her fairies flew around during that magical period between dark and the first peep of the sun on the horizon. Guiltily, Dennis slunk down in his chair.

Heidi's ruined skin continued to heal, but a uniform whiteness did not return. Instead, she ended up with red splotches in visible and unusual places. Heidi was undaunted by this change in color. After her forced nakedness, Heidi had lost all capacity to be embarrassed by her appearance.

Having a grown woman in the house produced change. Heidi instituted rules about dirty boots in the house, daily sweeping of the floor, ash removal from the fireplace, and a host of other rules.

The men had known greasy hermits and unwashed cowboys on the trail, but it never dawned on them to consider they might themselves be dirty. Heidi had the gall to make them increase their number of baths from one a month to one a week. Kel refused until Heidi told him she would remove his clothes and bathe him herself. Well, Heidi may have gotten used to being naked around us, but the thought of taking our clothes off in front of her caused us to run.

No one felt confident leaving the house. For a week everyone hunkered down. Unfortunately, the pasture next to the barn was not meant to sustain so many horses for so long. After much discussion, it was decided the eleven Comanche ponies would be set loose in the morning. If the ponies decided to return to the other horses by dusk, they would be let back in the pasture for collective protection.

The Comanche ponies came back that night and the next. At this point, the decision was made to let several of the other horses loose to further reduce the pressure on the pasture. Additional horses were let loose each morning, but four were always kept in the pasture in case we had to search for the other horses.

Since we had not had a frost yet, I recommended we take the wagon out and collect as much of the grass south of the canyon as possible. Every day for a week we harvested the buffalograss, yellow indiangrass, little bluestem, and sideoats grama until the hayloft above the stone barn was packed tighter than a preacher's purse.

Having hay was important as a last resort. Horses when left to their own devices, would eat twenty or more pounds of grass a day. If we had to keep them in the barn for very long we needed something to feed them.

The problem was not only the hay going in, but the hay coming out. Depending on the weight of the horse, a horse could produce twenty or more pounds of manure a day. We needed to keep the manure from flowing into the dammed water and fouling it. Each day we took turns shoveling out the barn and picking up manure in the pasture. We loaded the horse manure in the wagon and drove it down to a nice meadow where the manure could fertilize what someday would be a hay pasture.

Being more of a calendar person than any other of the others, I surprised them when I pointed out tomorrow was Christmas. For better or worse, Kara had four fathers. Each of us felt the importance of teaching Kara about Christmas. Kel looked through the surrounding woods and found a six-foot cedar tree that with a bit of trimming was a passable Christmas tree. Hiding the tree in the barn, Dennis and Heidi attached bits of shiny rocks and colored leather strips to the tree. Darryl carved a star and secured it on the top.

Each of us disappeared at some point in the day as we secretly created gifts for Kara. Christmas morning I presented Kara with a wooden carving of Kit. Darryl gave Kara a beautiful hat of rabbit fur he painfully sewed himself. Dennis, like some doting mother, had sewn a beautiful pair of moccasins decorated with fairies. Kel presented Kara with a pail filled to the rim with a fresh honeycomb.

To Heidi's delight, we had taken some of Kel's soft pelts and sewn together moccasins for her, and a top with thin leather strings hanging from the arms that made a sound like wind swishing through the trees. When presented with her gifts, Heidi rubbed them lovingly against her skin and moaned not from pain, but with pleasure.

Surrounded by presents, we took turns telling Kara about Christmas, God, Jesus, a father's love for his son, and us. Kara stared at each of us for a long period and turned to Dennis whispering, "Is Jesus a fairy?"

• • •

Several weeks of shoring up our defenses and rechecking our boundaries left us restless and eager to implement the gold plan agreed upon eight months ago. Inventing a chore to get Heidi out of the house, I sent her and Kara off to the creek to catch some fish for dinner.

I said, "I don't like keeping secrets from Heidi, but I am uncertain whether we are ready to share our secrets just yet."

Nods affirmed agreement. Dennis stuttered, "Uh, I don't want Heidi to know I am rich. If she decides to stay, I want it to be because she, uh, likes me as a cowboy."

Everyone laughed. Dennis's face and neck flushed beat red. I said, "Cowboy, that girl loves you. I do not think we could drive her away with sticks. When you decide to tell Heidi just let us know so that we can account for everyone who knows about the gold."

"Now back to business. We must time our actions. Once word gets out about the gold, our area will be flooded with gold seekers. Kel and Darryl, return home and pay everyone twice the value of the vouchers you obtained. Get a signed receipt for each voucher. We will give you travel time and two days to hand out the gold. I will try to time it so that I arrive in Austin with as much gold as the wagon can safely carry the same day you arrive."

"Copying the Austin shopkeeper's idea, I have modified the wagon by replacing some of the heavy oak timbers with bamboo so that it weighs less. I figure the wagon can carry twelve hundred pounds of gold. This may be our only chance to safely transport gold, so I am also going to trail two of the bigger horses behind the wagon with two hundred pounds of gold each. That should roughly be half a million in gold."

"We need to prepare for the worse, which is somebody taking our land and the money we put in the bank. When you boys go back to Waller, take two Comanche ponies each. Put one hundred and fifty pounds of gold on each pony. Find a good place, bury the gold, and sell the ponies. The day may come where that six hundred pounds of gold is our last chance money."

"When we meet in Austin, Darryl will guard the wagon while I open bank accounts in our names. Kel will take our legal documents to a lawyer. After the bank deposits, we will drive the wagon to the land office and buy as much land as the remaining gold allows."

"Then we will drive the wagon to the mercantile store and fill our supply list. Darryl, see if you can buy another wagon and a team to pull it. If you can quickly purchase the wagon, then double the supply order. You two will drive those wagons back home as quickly as possible."

"Before we depart I will give the storekeeper enough gold to purchase three more wagons full of goods. Leave it to the storekeeper to hire drivers to deliver the goods. Once word of the gold gets out we may be in danger anytime we leave our land."

"Dennis, your job is to protect Kara and keep anyone from showing up and taking over the mine while we are gone."

Everyone nodded somberly at each other. Things were about to get dangerous. A good chance existed that people were going to try and kill us for the gold.

Texas was a young Republic with a small population. More coyotes and wolves were in Texas than people. Some of the coyotes were on two legs and would kill you for a horse, even more so for a horse packing gold.

"Darryl and Kel, try to time it right, no messing around this time. I figure it should take y'all ten maybe eleven days to get to Waller, two days to pay off the land, and six days to travel to Austin for a total of eighteen or so days. Since it will take me around fifteen days to get to Austin with the heavy wagon and gold, I will leave Lost Maples several days after y'all depart."

With a heaviness in my heart, I turned to everyone and said, "We need to do more with our gold than just get rich. Each of us has friends who lost an arm or a leg in the Revolution. The Republic of Texas granted each of them a Military Headright land grant of 4,428 acres, but as we all know, there is not enough cash to make a go of the land.[1] I propose we establish a Republic of Texas fund to help them."

Nodding their heads, Kel, Dennis, and Darryl agreed.

Turning to Kel, I said, "When you get to Austin have the lawyer put together paperwork for such a fund."

• • •

The next morning, January 18, 1841, Kel and Darryl were up early, arranging and rearranging the weight of the gold on the pack horses. When convinced the weight could be carried comfortably, they tightened the cinches on their saddle horses and set off for Waller.

Tension weighed heavy in the air the first day the boys were gone. Dennis and I talked about deer tracks, wolves, the state of the horses, everything except what occupied our thoughts, the safety of Kel and Darryl.

On January 20, the day before my departure, I was up early drinking coffee when Kara swung down from the ladder where we slept and laid her head against my side. I hugged Kara, and she began to cry. Kit who was almost a year old, glided over to Kara anxiously looking back and forth between Kara and me. With a loud "mrrr" Kit plopped her body down in Kara's lap completely covering Kara and flowing several feet of cougar on either side.

Hugging them both tightly, I said, "Kara honey, it will take me fifteen days or so to travel to Austin and six days back."

Picking up my hand, Kara began to count my fingers. Lifting the thumb, she said, "One, two, five, six."

We were teaching Kara to count. I laughed, and we practiced counting until with a combination of her hands and mine we reached twenty-one. We repeated counting to twenty-one until I thought my hair would fall out.

Dennis saved me by walking up and saying, "While Rye is gone, Kara and I will practice our gazintas and tutums."[2]

I laughed and my puzzlement must have shown on my face.

Dennis responded, "You know, three gazinta six twice and tutumis four is eight."

NOTES

1. Texas General Land Office, "Categories of Land Grants," accessed April 5, 2018, www.glo.texas.gov/history/archives/forms/files/glo-headright-military-land-grants.pdf.

2. Walton, *Bear Meat 'n' Honey*, 19. This counting method was shared in *Bear Meat 'n' Honey* by Oma Highsmith Jones Lewis who was born in 1903 three miles northwest of Utopia which is fifteen miles south of Lost Maples.

CHAPTER TWENTY

I awoke long before the faintest glow appeared in the east. In order not to wake Heidi, I prodded Dennis with my hand, pointing to the door to indicate I was leaving. Kara was still asleep, so I gently hugged her. I stroked Kit's soft ears and gently closed the door behind me. My departure was quiet, I hoped the ranch remained that way during my absence.

Traveling to Austin my preference would have been to ride Woe and trail a pack horse. Instead, I was driving a wagon full of gold and trailing two heavily loaded pack horses. I felt naked. For safety, I followed the landscape closely, keeping off the high ground to avoid being profiled. Texas was a beautiful but wild country. The Comanche, Apache, Kiowa, Waco, and a half-dozen other tribes posed a danger. Unfortunately, just as dangerous were the white men who had gone bad. These bad white men would enter your camp under the pretense to share your food and drink your coffee. Afterward, they would feel little hesitation to kill you and steal everything you owned.

A constant state of vigilance was required. I dared not risk a fire and had to dry camp. Each night I slept uncomfortably outside the camp while leaving behind a bedroll filled with grass to serve as a convenient target.

Three days out of Lost Maples I came across a trail made by unshod ponies traveling west to east. They were not a danger to me unless by sheer bad luck they happened to return the exact moment we were traveling home. Life on the frontier was a game of chance.

Two days from Austin I saw shod horse tracks, some single horses, some in pairs. If the tracks were any indication, the young town of Austin was becoming a busy place.

With relief the next day I camped out an hour from Austin. I planned to reach town just after sunrise.

The following morning, with a narrow slice of yellow showing on the horizon, I hitched up the wagon and headed into town. It was only February of 1841 and Austin had grown much larger since my last visit. The population was around eight hundred last year, and now it looked double that if not more.

Could a year have passed? There were several new saloons and shacks around the edges of town. The main street was lined with new banks, mercantile stores, and office buildings for the Republic of Texas. Austin exuded an air of importance.

I passed the Ranger Headquarters and on impulse turned around and tied the team to the railing. Feeling slightly less hesitant than last time, I walked through the door and asked, "Good Morning, is Captain Eldridge available?"

Hearing his name, Captain Eldridge appeared as though having been waiting for his name to be called. "Good morning, Rye. Almost a year has passed. Did you decide to take up Rangering?"

"Good morning sir, can we speak privately in your office?"

Captain Eldridge led me into a spartan room with a battered desk, two chairs, and an assortment of rifles in cases against the wall. Being a man of few words, he simply stared at me, waiting for me to begin.

"Several months after that shooting with the three outlaws, two hard cases showed up at my property looking for the man who kills outlaws."

Captain Eldridge nodded. "Where did you bury them?"

"Uh, I did not bury them. I took their guns and sent them on their way."

The Ranger stared as he had on our first meeting and simply said, "Start at the beginning."

I retold my encounter with the outlaws from Woe's warning to their quick departure. It might have been my imagination, but I thought I detected faint traces of a smile on Captain Eldridge's face. Standing to let me know our time was up, he said, "Next time bury them."

With a tinge of sadness, I said, "Our ranch was raided by Comanche three times since I saw you last. The first time I was alone. I killed two and my horse killed two."

Captain Eldridge laughed and said, "Remind me to avoid your horse."

"The second time I had my brother Darryl, cousin Dennis, and friend Kel with me. We buried eight Comanche. Unfortunately, we also buried eight Karankawa we had given permission to camp on our ranch. The decision was unlucky for them."

"Our third fight with the Comanche we killed six at the ranch. We chased them for two days and then they chased us for a day. In the end, we must have killed three dozen or more of the Comanche. They made the mistake of hitting our ranch when they were out of gunpowder and almost out of arrows."

"We killed a lot of Comanche, but in the chase, we came across several captives. One, a boy of seven or eight, was already dead, it looked like he was thrown or fell from a horse. The other was a young woman named Sarah McCullough who we came across as she was dying of a broken back. We took their bodies home with us and gave them a proper burial."

"During the chase, we also came across a seventeen-year-old girl named Heidi whose family was massacred. Heidi decided to stay with us."

With a softness I had not expected, Captain Eldridge said, "Start from the beginning, please."

I retold the story from beginning to end and Captain Eldridge nodded to indicate he had heard enough. Hesitantly I stood up, but then sat back down. "I am afraid there is going to be trouble and I thought you should know."

The Ranger lowered himself back down to his seat and watched my face for several minutes. "Continue," he said.

"That wagon parked in front of Ranger Headquarters is full of gold. I will be putting that gold in four banks and buying more land around my gold mine at Lost Maples."

To my surprise, Captain Eldridge smiled and said, "That makes my job easier. I do not have to hunt outlaws anymore. They will come to me right here in Austin. After we thin them out, the survivors will likely head down to your mine."

The Ranger then sat and stared at me a full two minutes before he spoke again. "After we have thinned them out up here, I will send a couple of Rangers down to your ranch. When the time comes, they may need to swear you and your partners in as temporary Rangers." For the first time, his voice had an edge to it as he said, "This is not a request. Is that understood?"

With a shiver running down my back, I said, "Yes sir." Without another word, he stood up and strode to the door where he called out, "Sam."

A slight fellow, weighing no more than a fence post stepped up and saluted. The Captain said, "Sam, guard the contents of this young man's wagon while he is in town. Do not let that wagon leave your sight."

The young Ranger had a puzzled look on his face but did not ask any questions or say anything in response. He simply walked outside and sat on the wagon's front bench.

I walked outside expecting to find a sullen Ranger waiting for me. Instead, he smiled and extended his hand, "Howdy, you can call me Sam."

Extending my hand, I said, "Rye."

Sam smiled broadly and asked, "Are you offering me whiskey?"

"Uh no, that is my name. Unfortunately, there is no time for whiskey today. I am meeting my partners. We are going to the land office, bank, lawyer, land office, and then the mercantile, but I will stand you one next time I see you."

Sam smiled as though he did not have a care in the world. To my surprise, he never inquired about the wagon's contents nor what made me so important I needed Ranger protection. We drove up to the land office where I got down while Sam settled onto the wagon seat.

Strolling in the door, Professor Eldridge immediately recognized me. "Howdy Lost Maples, how is your land treating you? I hope your friends found you ok?"

Smiling at his friendly greeting I responded, "Thanks professor, they did. We plan to buy more land. Will you be open all day?"

"Certainly. But call me Zeke."

"Would you mind pulling out your survey maps for my area? We made minor corrections to the maps laying out our previous land purchases." I laid out the original maps with their corrections, showing the five-thousand-acre plots owned by the four of us separately, our homesteads, and the boundaries of our jointly held land.

Zeke nodded approvingly, "I will make the corrections in duplicate like before. I can add the boundaries of the new land purchases while I am at it if you want?"

"Making the changes now would save time. I suspect we will want to leave town quickly." Stretching out the largest map, I quickly outlined the new land purchase. I wanted the land stretching from the mouth of the canyon, south to where the canyon walls drifted several miles apart. The land in between was a flat valley full of tall grass, with the Sabinal River a mere two-foot creek running up against one of the canyon walls.

"Rye, if I remember correctly, that is good ranch land. Are you sure you want this boundary? You are talking about adding another one hundred and fifty thousand acres."

"That is right," I was tempted to say more but held back.

"After buying supplies and making a bank deposit, I will be back to pay for the land." Walking out the door, I could feel Zeke's unspoken questions hanging in the air.

I plopped down in the wagon seat with a sigh. Turning to Sam I said, "Can you offer me an opinion on the banks in town?"

Winking his right eye, Sam said, "Don't tell anyone I told you, but Barons will rob you. Tillerson's is shaky, and Lincrest's an unknown. Your best bets are the Bank of Texas, the Republic Bank, First National, or the Dietrich Bank. The others are still too new for me to have an opinion about."

"Do you have any opinions about the lawyers in town?"

The Ranger smiled and said, "One lawyer is too many. The most honest of the bunch used to be a Texas Ranger so you can trust him. His name is Shanty Voelkel."

Before I could turn the team around two dusty cowboys pulled up to the wagon. I could feel the electricity sparking from Sam as his hand slid toward his gun.

In alarm, I said, "Sam, I would like for you to meet my partners Kel and Darryl." Instantly Sam transformed back into the easy-going young man I originally met. I had seriously misjudged Sam. Captain Eldridge had given me a deadly guardian.

"Kel, Darryl, this is Sam. Captain Eldridge was kind enough to allow Sam here to stay with the wagon while we conduct our business today."

"Stroke of luck," Darryl said. Kel just looked from Sam to me and back.

With a big grin, Darryl said, "Kel recognized the wagon the minute we got into town."

I nodded, "Any problems?"

"None we couldn't handle. But we need to take care of business and get on our way."

The grimness on both their faces conveyed a lot had transpired that was better said later. "I found four reputable banks, let's get it done. Kel, Shanty Voelkel is the lawyer recommended to us. He used to be a Ranger. See if you can locate him and get our documents legally recognized."

Leaving Sam to watch the wagon and its gold, Darryl and I took two saddlebags each into the First National Bank and asked to see the manager. He glanced at our battered hats and dusty chaps and motioned an assistant to take care of us. I shook my head and motioned toward his private office. With an exasperated sigh, he waved off the assistant and headed to his office.

With a fake smile oozing smug disapproval the manager asked, "How might I assist you, gentlemen?"

The slimy way he said gentleman was mighty irksome. Controlling my irritation, I said, "We would like to open an account."

With an exasperated sigh, he asked, "How much would you like to deposit?"

Nonchalantly I replied, "Sixty thousand."

With a bewildered look at us, he repeated, "Sixty thousand?"

I dropped a saddlebag on his desk with a jarring thud and pulled out a handful of the melted gold. Pointing to the saddlebag on his desk and the other one on the floor, I said, "Those should weigh roughly two hundred pounds."

"Sir, I cannot accept your gold. For all I know, you robbed a bank to get it."

I smiled knowingly. "I represent a corporation that owns a gold mine. Reaching inside the saddlebag on the floor I pulled out a handful of the gold-lined quartz. We are opening accounts in four of Austin's finest banks. If you are reluctant to accept our gold, we will happily place it with one of your competitors." I buckled up the saddlebag and got up as if to leave.

The banker responded with a smile I once saw on a heehawing jackass who curled his lips back to reveal every tooth in his head. "Sir, perhaps I misspoke. We would be happy to open an account." Leaning out his door he yelled, "Jenkins, bring the large weight scales into my office."

A thin man with lips pursed in disapproval returned several minutes later hauling in a scale his bony arms could barely manage. The gold was quickly weighed and came out to be two hundred and two pounds and one ounce. At 18.93 dollars an ounce, that came to a deposit of 61,163 dollars. The account was opened in all four of our names.

With a smile, the banker said, "Sir, that figure is just a rough estimate. The purity of the gold must be assayed for an accurate number."

With a knowing smile, I said, "We will be opening accounts at three other banks today. Future deposits will depend on the accuracy of such an assay."

"Yes, yes, of course," said the banker as his face flushed at being put on notice no shenanigans would be tolerated.

In short order, we had six bank accounts opened at four banks. A joint account in all our names and four individual accounts worth three hundred and twenty thousand dollars total. A sixth account was opened as a fund for injured veterans of the Texas Revolution.

Darryl and I signed the joint account and our separate accounts and informed them Kel would be by momentarily. We told the bankers Dennis was the fourth person and he would be in within the year to sign for himself.

By the time the last account was opened, activity swirled outside the bank as people rushed back and forth reverently whispering the word gold. When Kel returned from the lawyer he added his signature to both the joint account and his individual account.

Glancing warily at Kel and Darryl. I said, "Forget the plan about driving the wagons back. Kel, go to the mercantile, grab stuff you can put on each of the horses for a quick trip home. Give the mercantile our supply list. Tell him to quadruple our order, including the ammunition. Also, ask him to buy or rent us four wagons and their teams to haul the goods to Lost Maples. Ask him to hire drivers and pay double what they typically would make. Tell him we will bring over a fifth wagon that is already ours. Pay him to fill it with goods and to hire a driver to follow the other four drivers."

Kel nodded approvingly. "Five wagons of supplies should guarantee we don't have to leave the ranch until things settle down."

Turning to Darryl, I said, "Since I am leaving the wagon, I will ride home on the two horses I trailed behind the wagon on the trip to Austin. I intended to sell them, but now I need to ride them back. I hate to say it since we already have too many horses, but I think you will also need two horses apiece to beat this crowd home. Darryl, pay whatever you must. Purchase a second horse for each of you with all the tack and get tack for my two horses. Sam and I are headed to the land office. Be ready to go in ten minutes."

I climbed into the wagon and drove straight to the General Land Office. Upon entering, I closed and locked the door. Glancing out the window I placed a closed sign in the window.

Zeke grinned and said "Rye" in a way that my name sounded like a question.

Grinning I said, "I would like to purchase those one hundred and fifty thousand acres I mentioned earlier."

The professor nodded, "That is a lot of land. At seventy cents an acre that will roughly run you one hundred and five thousand dollars."

With a sly grin, I said, "Lost Maples has a gold mine."

Laughing he said, "You do realize, there are no gold mines in Texas?"

Plopping my saddlebag onto the large map table, I pulled out a bag of the gold-veined quartz and spread its contents on his desk. I then dumped out several of the gold clumps we had melted down.

I repeated, "Lost Maples has a gold mine." I pointed at the melted gold and said, "Five pounds of this is a fee for you. In my wagon is enough gold to buy the land I mentioned. Help me do this as quickly as possible before the rush starts."

Smiling he said, "You seemed so intent when you arrived this morning that while you were gone I took the liberty of adding the land you requested. Zeke pulled out newly drawn maps in which one hundred and fifty thousand acres had been added. The new maps contained more precise locations for canyons, hills, and stream beds on our previously purchased land. He had added our boundary stakes for the homesteads, the five thousand acres plots for each of us, the boundary for the initial one hundred and twenty thousand acres, as well as the boundaries for the newest one hundred and fifty thousand acres.

I showed Zeke the legal document drawn up by Kel about our individual and joint land. On the maps, he indicated our individual and joint ownership. "Like before, one copy goes to you, one to the General Land Office, and one to the Archives Office. You mentioned three partners earlier, so I made up three spare maps for your partners. I also made out one for you to give to a lawyer, I suspect you may need one. I know you are in a hurry, but quickly check to make sure there are no errors."

My heart was pounding. I needed to get out of there, but a mistake at this point could be very costly. Forcing myself to slow down, I focused on each detail of the map, pointing out several small changes which were quickly corrected. When we both agreed the seven maps were identical, a sigh of relief escaped from both our lips. With relish, we both signed the maps and dated them, February 5, 1841.

"Where do you want me to stack the gold for the land?"

Alarmed, Zeke said, "For heaven's sake don't leave it here. Within the hour I would be robbed and laying dead on the floor. I will ride with you to the Republic of Texas Bank where you can deposit it in the General Land Office account."

When I unlocked the door, I found Sam with his gun out telling people to stay away from the wagon. A big brute of a fella ignored the warning and reached to move a corner of the canvas covering the back of the wagon. Sam's shot sprayed wooden splinters on the unbeliever's hand and forearm.

With dead earnest, Sam said, "Touch that wagon again and you lose a finger. Touch your gun and lose your life." Growling the big guy backed up as did the rest of the crowd.

The land agent and I hurriedly stepped aboard while Sam climbed into the back. We drove to the bank, weaving around the crowd building up in the street.

Upon reaching the Republic of Texas Bank, Zeke and I walked in carrying saddlebags which we plopped down on the floor. We made several more trips while Professor Eldridge explained to the bank manager the money was going into the Republic of Texas General Land Office account.

I looked at the bank manager. "Weigh it out now before we have a riot."

Closing the bank doors, they weighed out the gold and found we were ten thousand dollars over. Nonchalantly I said, "Add it to the sixty thousand I deposited earlier."

Hurriedly Professor Eldridge wrote out seven duplicate receipts showing the land was paid in full. He shook my hand and said, "I hope you get home safely. God bless."

Before heading out the door, I retrieved some papers from my jacket and handed them to Zeke. "Your book has been especially useful. I took notes about the types of trees and brush in Lost Maples. I added some information about medicine plants shared with us by a group of Karankawa."

Zeke's beaming smile made all the note-taking worthwhile. With a wave, I walked out the door to confront a shouting crowd. Swarming like angry ants, they were no longer whispering gold, they were shouting it. I turned to Kel who was holding the reins of a beautiful bay horse whose red coat gave rise to its more common name, a blood bay. With a look of guilt on his face, Darryl held the reins of a magnificent pinto with large patches of black, brown, and white.

Rushing to justify his purchase, Darryl blurted out, "Since I knew we would have to overpay, I went ahead and got horses we could breed. Do not say it. Yes, I paid three times their worth. Let's drop the wagon and team off at the mercantile and ride like hell out of here."

I knew we desperately needed to escape Austin, but when we got to the mercantile, I stopped outside the door. Taking a deep breath I slowly pushed the door open.

Kel and Darryl were bewildered by my lack of urgency. Their mouths opened and shut without saying a word.

Approaching the counter, I removed my hat and stared at the red-haired young woman. "Yes," she said, drawing out the word as though it had ten letters.

"Um, I would like to speak to your father to square up my account," I stammered.

She threw back her shoulders, "Unlike you, my father believes a woman is perfectly capable of handling business. I can square your account."

My face turned bright red, and I heard laughter behind me.

Looking over my shoulder and back to my face, she asked, "Are these gentlemen with you?"

"Uh, yes."

"They made sizeable purchases. Our store policy is that delinquent accounts must be paid in full before new purchases can be made. Your account has been short for almost a year."

With embarrassment, I said, "Yes ma'am. I am here to square the account and pay any interest due."

Making a tsking sound, she shook her head and said, "You should have said so."

Darryl burst into loud guffaws and slapped me on the back.

Smooth with women, Darryl stepped forward and said, "Ma'am, please forgive my brother Rye. His head gets thick and his tongue swells around beautiful women."

This admission brought a smile to the storekeeper's daughter as she looked from Darryl to me. "Thank you for introducing your brother. We met last year but he failed to properly introduce himself or share his name."

"My name is Rye," I offered with a weak smile.

"Do you have a drinking problem?" she asked.

Bewildered, I shook my head no. "Then why are you named after whiskey?" she asked.

"Ma'am, it's a long story," I stupidly offered.

Darryl shook his head and stifled a laugh. With a bow, Darryl said, "Ma'am, may we have the pleasure of knowing your name?"

With a curtsy, she said, "Mary Elizabeth O'Shay, but my friends call me Tib."

Darryl turned to me and with exaggerated formality said, "Rye, please allow me to introduce Miss Tib O'Shay."

My ears burned red. I felt as though all the blood in my body was throbbing in my face. Gulping, I said as calmly as possible, "I believe this should cover the cost of the credit your store was so kind to extend me when I first visited Austin. My friends have arranged and paid for five wagons of supplies, as well as four of the wagons and teams to transport them."

Losing my nerve, I began to stutter and barely got out, "I would like to leave a deposit with you to cover future expenses." In embarrassment, I plopped a bag of gold on the counter and slunk out.

I learned later our departure left Austin in chaos. Bank customers and tellers quickly spread tidbits of information that grew with each telling. By the end of the day, it was rumored we deposited over a million dollars of gold in every bank in Austin. Our names were cursed by banks in the weeks to come. Captain Eldridge's prediction rang true as every thief and crook within the Republic of Texas was drawn to Austin to rob the banks of their gold bullion.

Buying our five wagon loads of supplies before the rumors got out proved wise. That day people rushed to the land office to buy land next to Lost Maples in a feverish dream to own a gold mine. There was a run on every mercantile in town. Wagons, teams, and supplies went for two, three, and then ten times their worth. A wagon train of people filled with gold lust was headed our way.

CHAPTER TWENTY-ONE

Glancing from one face to another, I recognized a shared sense of urgency as we departed Austin. The four hours we spent getting our affairs in order, was time those with ill intent might use to their advantage. Initially, the ride was a little awkward with each of us trailing a second saddle horse, but we got the hang of it. Riding hard and switching horses quickly, there was no time to talk.

With our late start, we only made fifteen miles on the first day. Though no one caught up to us, there was always the chance someone was just waiting for us to let our guard down. Each night we camped out away from the trail and without a fire. Nothing gets a cowboy down like cold coffee.

Bedding down the second night, Darryl and Kel caught me up on the news that was seven months old but had not reached us in Lost Maples. Speaking in low voices, they shared Chief Buffalo Hump had gathered warriors from many Comanche camps, inflaming warriors with blood lust after the March 1840 Council House betrayal. The chief and what was believed to be between six hundred and a thousand Comanche stormed across Texas, raiding as far as the Texas coast in what was being referred to as the Great Raid of 1840.[1] On August the sixth, the Comanche swarmed over Victoria and two days later they attacked Linnville. The number of isolated settlers and unfortunate travelers killed by the Comanche was unknown, but several dozen townspeople died during the Victoria-Linnville raids.[2]

The Comanche, typically known for their lighting raids, were slowed down to a plodding pace as they hauled away a massive amount of goods stolen from the port at Linnville. This slow pace allowed Texas militia volunteers under Ed Burleson from Bastrop and Mathew Caldwell from Gonzales to combine with several Ranger companies to catch up and defeat the Comanche on August twelfth at Plum Creek near Lockhart.[3]

When Darryl and Kel finished their story, Kel cautioned, "Though that was seven months ago, there are still scattered bands of Comanche raiding. They are still plenty upset. We must always be on our guard. The chance for peace with the Comanche in Texas has been lost."

Riding and sleeping while remaining vigilant is exhausting, so it was with relief at the end of the fifth day when we saw the outline of our home. Our jubilation diminished as we drew closer. No smoke danced from the chimney and there were strange horses in the pasture.

Out of caution we circled from a distance. Though Dennis had resisted the idea, we convinced him to move into the smaller house while we were gone. The small house above the mine was easier for one person to defend.

No activity or sound came from the small house or the newer large house. The rifle ports revealed no movement, and no rifle barrels were visible.

We tied off the horses by the well up the slope from the house. With a mixture of caution and worry, we quietly crept up to the dwelling. Our backs to the stone walls, I stretched upward and called softly, "Dennis" several times. The third time we received a faint response.

"Who is there?"

"It's us, Rye, Darryl, and Kel."

The barely audible voice inside whispered, "Come around to the front and step away from the door so I can see you."

I walked around to the front of the house, stepping away from the front door. Up above me, I could see Dennis peeking out through one of the rifle ports and Heidi poking a rifle out of another. We heard someone climb down the ladder, lift the bar from the door, and swing it open. A haggard-looking Dennis stood in the doorway.

"I am glad to see you, boys."

Darryl said, "Looks like you had a hard time of it."

Dennis nodded his head wearily, "Now that you boys are home we can make a fire. I sorely need some hot coffee."

No one spoke as we all eagerly chipped in to get the coffee going. Kel gathered tinder and wood for a fire. Darryl placed two handfuls of coffee beans into a burlap sack and pounded the beans into coffee grounds. Dennis dipped a pitcher into the cistern and poured the water into our battered tin coffee pot.

With nothing to do but wait for the coffee to boil, everyone settled down around the fireplace as Dennis related his story. "When you said I had to remain here and protect the gold mine, I thought you were just joshing me so that I would not protest being left behind. I am ashamed to admit I was not overly vigilant and became less so the longer y'all were gone."

"Moving into your old house because it was easier to defend seemed unnecessary. We moved, but I was not happy about it."

"Late yesterday afternoon, Kara and I were in the house starting to make dinner while Heidi was taking a nap. Suddenly two outlaws burst through the door with guns drawn. Kara happened to be close to the door. Reaching out, an outlaw grabbed Kara by the arm and jerked her off the ground. Little Kara started screaming bloody murder."

"Kit had been sleeping on Rye's platform to the right of the door. Before I knew what was happening, seven feet of riled-up cougar leaped from the platform. A hundred and fifty pounds of rage hit the outlaw in the back as Kit sunk her teeth just below the skull snapping the startled outlaw's neck. Before his body even hit the ground, Kit let go and ripped the other outlaw's arm and belly open with her claws. I kicked the man's rifle away as the horrified outlaw's guts tumbled out of his body."

"Barring the door, I quickly climbed the ladder. From the rifle port, I could see two men down by the fake gold mine. I debated shooting them if they drew near the house, but what if they had nothing to do with the attack? Now that I say it out loud, I know how foolish it sounds. All the same, I could not just shoot them without being sure."

"Hugging Kara, I sent her and Kit up the ladder to your corner. Heidi refused to go."

"I dragged the bodies away from the door and threw a blanket over them. Unbarring the front door, Heidi and I turned over the big oak table and crouched down behind it with several rifles and pistols."

"I figured if the men rode up to the house and called out for the other two, they were outlaws. If they came through the door without knocking, they were outlaws. But if they knocked and called out, I would just ignore them and see what happened."

"They removed all doubt by walking in the door with guns drawn without any greeting. I shot the first outlaw twice with my Paterson. One bullet hit him in the belly and the second hit him in the chest. The second bullet must have hit a rib because it tore a groove in his chest and hit him in the jaw. He fell back screaming."

"Not letting them both in before I started shooting was a mistake. The second outlaw used his friend's body as cover while backing out the front door. While he scrambled backward Heidi shot him in the thigh. Bleeding like a stuck pig the outlaw threw his rifle down and raised his hands in surrender."

"I give up, I give up," he cried.

"You know how your pa's pigs bled when we hung them up by their hind legs and cut their throats during the fall butchering? That is how this fella bled. His thigh was bubbling like a red fountain and squirting blood a foot in the air. You would swear someone had thrown a bucket of water onto him, only it was blood."

The outlaw said in a whiny voice, "Aren't you going to help me?"

I just stared at him. "You came to kill us. No one can help you. Another minute and all your blood will be in the dirt."

"Sure enough, in a minute his leg stopped spurting. Though sunburned, the man's face turned white, and then grey. The outlaw's chest stopped heaving and his eyes clouded."

"I could not chance being caught alone outdoors burying them, so the four bodies are stacked next to the barn. If it were not for Kit, you would be burying our bodies."

Everyone took turns walking over and giving Kit hugs and thanking her for saving Kara. Though only thirteen months old, at one and fifty pounds, Kit was already bigger than most full-grown female cougars who reached their top size at fifteen months. Kit stood three feet high at the shoulders with a seven-foot-long frame, three feet of that length being her long tawny tail.

Most cougars lived a life of feast and famine, living off rodents, raccoons, rabbits, squirrels, possums, and if lucky, a deer every two weeks. Since she was six months old, Kit had supplied a lot of her own food, but we kept her constantly filled with the meat we ate. Being almost full-grown, Kit ate between eight and ten pounds of meat whenever she joined us for a meal. Kit had a constant supply of food that encouraged growth a wild cougar could not sustain.

Kel, ever the practical one, put down his coffee cup and said, "Let's bury those outlaws before they get too ripe."

While Kel and I dug the graves, Darryl kept watch. I drew the faces of the men we were burying. On the next trip to Austin, I could share the drawings with the Rangers. Going through their pockets we were unable to find anything indicating their names. We did find that each man had five twenty-dollar gold pieces in their pockets.

Someone paid these thieves a hundred dollars apiece to steal our mine. We figured we spent four hours in Austin. No one passed us on the trail. To get ahead of us they must have left Austin within an hour of our arrival. Someone knew to send these men straight to Lost Maples. The fact that someone could react that fast and have ready money to pay the outlaws, hinted at a level of organization that did not bode well for us. A crooked banker or a well-organized outlaw group was already operating in Austin. Either way, we were going to always have a gun handy and treat every stranger as though they were a killer.

We added their four rifles and two pistols to our growing arsenal. Few of the guns we were collecting from Indians and outlaws were quality pieces, but we could use them for parts.

One of the pistols was of a better quality than you would expect on an outlaw. The gun was a Johnson Model 1836 single-shot flintlock pistol made for the American government. Five years ago, when new, the pistols sold for nine dollars apiece.[4] The almost nine-inch barrel fired a hefty .45 caliber slug. Made you wonder how bottom dwellers like these got such guns?

They also had one worn-out Henry Model 1813 Navy pistol. This .54 caliber single-shot muzzle loading flintlock pistol was originally made for the American Navy.[5] The pistol had seen a lot of use and appeared worn to the point where you used it at your peril.

The outlaws had one worn-out Brown Bess, two decent ones, and a fourth that was broken. There were two Kentucky rifles, one inlaid with silver engraving that must have been stolen off someone wealthy. The second Kentucky rifle was plain, and the type typically used for hunting.

Two of the eight outlaw horses were quality animals. One was a dun-colored Mustang and the other a buckskin gelding. Mustang was a name given to the descendants of wild horses. Having to feed and protect themselves, mustangs were tough horses with staying quality.

Of the other six horses, none was of high quality and they had been ridden to the point of almost breaking them down. With these recent additions, we now had twenty-three animals. We had too much livestock for our small-fenced pasture.

Taking the animals to new areas to feed was going to be dangerous in the coming months. Each of us needed spare animals, and we needed quality breeding stock. But not as many as we currently owned. When the wagons with our supplies arrived, we would arrange for the muleskinners to take some of the horses back with them. In the meantime, we would have to go back to setting most of the horses out to graze on their own during the day. Hopefully, they would return for the night.

NOTES

1. Handbook *of Texas Online*, Craig H. Roell, "Linnville Raid of 1840," accessed May 14, 2018, https://www.tshaonline.org/handbook/online/articles/btl01.

2. Ibid.

3. Wikipedia, "Battle of Plum Creek," accessed April 17, 2018, https://en.wikipedia.org/wiki/Battle_of_Plum_Creek.

4. Military Factory, "Johnson Model 1836," accessed April 14, 2018, https://www.militaryfactory.com/smallarms/detail.asp?smallarms_id=312.

5. Military Factory, "Henry Model 1813," accessed April 14, 2018, https://www.militaryfactory.com/smallarms/detail.asp?smallarms_id=804#performance.

CHAPTER TWENTY-TWO

Knowing the wagons would arrive a week after our return, we began preparing for the incoming supplies. We decided to turn most of my original house into a supply depot lined with shelves. Kit kept the mice and rats in check, but some of the shelves would need to be enclosed to discourage the occasional survivor.

Felling the trees, trimming the logs, and building the shelving took us a week. During that time, no one else appeared at our door or the mine.

On the twenty-second of February, with the sun high overhead, five wagons filled with supplies rolled up to the house. I stood in the doorway to greet the wagons while barrels poked out the rifle ports overhead. If the wagons had been hijacked, there was no way we were going to be caught off guard.

Barking out, "Whoa mule," the dusty laden drivers engaged their brakes and hopped down, glad to be off the wagons. The mule drivers were all big, rough-looking men. I scanned their faces trying to identify which one was in charge.

Passing over their faces I was quickly drawn back to the face of a slender driver I barely recognized under the floppy hat and rough clothes. Yanking the hat off my head, I stepped forward and stammered, "Tib, what are you doing here?"

Removing her headgear and flapping it to get the dust off her hat and clothes, she smiled as though on an adventure. "Four wagons and teams, along with five wagons of supplies represent a huge investment on my father's part. If we lost these before delivery, it would set us back significantly, so my father sent me."

Before I could stop myself, I blurted out, "But, you are a girl."

Tib's countenance clouded over immediately. With a glare that could ignite a forest fire, through clenched teeth Tib said, "I am the best shot in my family and the most capable."

I hung my head in despair. Darryl hopped out the front door and slapped me on the back. "Howdy Tib. From the fire in your eyes and Rye's hangdog look, I can only guess he has stepped in it again. Allow me to welcome you to Lost Maples. Would you like a cup of coffee?"

The icy look on Tib's face thawed and she replied, "Let me take care of my men and animals first."

Kel walked out and said, "Tell your men to set the mules loose in the pasture next to the barn. The pasture is already chewed short, but they can graze there until you get them staked out. No need to water the mules, there is a dammed area in the pasture with water. The supplies can be unloaded in the center of the building next door, we will stock the shelves ourselves later."

"Tib, please warn your men not to make any sudden moves around our daughter Kara. Her guardian Kit has sharp teeth. Two men broke into the house several weeks ago. Kit snapped the neck of one and opened the other's belly so that it looked like a sack of wet snakes pouring out. Tell them if they pull a gun on Kit, we will kill them."

Both the harshness of Kel's tone and the content struck Tib as odd. A puzzled look crossed Tib's face as she tried to sort out what she had heard. None of the words made sense.

Hearing her name, Kit gracefully sauntered out the front door and sat down next to me. Tib and the mule drivers froze as the mules began braying wildly. I saw Tib closely examine Kit, her eyes fully taking in the tawny cougar who at fourteen months still had black spots faintly visible on the hind end of her seven-foot frame.

Tib knelt and without reaching out, softly said, "Hello Kit." To my surprise, Kit walked up to Tib and licked her chin, something Kit had never done.

Bearing a welcoming smile, Dennis walked out the door holding Kara in his arms. "Good morning, I am Dennis, and this is our daughter Kara."

If the cougar was a surprise, Kara was a shock. Looking from one man's face to the other, Tib detected no other information that would make sense of the situation. Nodding, Tib asked, "Are you Kara's father?"

"All of us are," we responded almost simultaneously.

Crouched on the ground with a hand on Kit's shoulder, Tib said, "Hello, Kara."

To this greeting, Kara looked away and buried her head in Dennis's shoulder. With an apologetic smile, Dennis said, "Don't mind Kara's manners ma'am. Several bad men treated Kara harshly two weeks ago. She is still a mite touchy around strangers."

"Poor child," said Tib. "Now I know why you ordered dress material. I thought it an odd thing for cowboys to buy."

"I won't push Kara, I will give her a chance to warm up to me." Turning to her men, Tib gathered them up and said, "See that young lady. Be kind and gentle with her. That cougar is her guardian and will tear you apart if she thinks you are threatening that child. See those four men, they said they will kill anyone who threatens that child or her cougar. I believe them. Put the mules in the pasture and stack the supplies in the center of the smaller stone house."

At this point, Heidi walked out of the house to stump Tib a third time. The assertive Heidi walked straight up to Tib and extended her hand. "I am Heidi."

Tib stammered, "Uh, Tib, nice to meet you." Walking away to supervise her men, Tib glanced uncertainly over her shoulder, struggling to understand Heidi's place on the ranch.

While the supplies were unloaded, Kel pulled half of a deer out of the cellar he had dug in the bigger house. When building the larger stone house, it had occurred to us it would be good to have a root cellar where coolness might keep vegetables and meat a little longer.

The smell of roasting venison filled the air as the afternoon passed. With the last supplies unloaded, the drivers were invited into the larger stone house where they sat down to a hot meal. Seated on the benches, chairs, and the floor, the mule drivers sucked the grease off their fingers as they gnawed on bones and chased the broiled venison down with gallons of coffee.

While eating dinner, the drivers recounted the anxiety they felt during the trip. One of the older drivers said, "The last week of the journey each of us had the eerie feeling of being watched. Fresh shod horse tracks were in the trail and we glimpsed single riders watching from ridges. Every night we slept with our rifles ready."

A second muleskinner added, "Four nights ago, Miss O'Shay insisted we start stopping for the night in places where fallen logs or rocks formed natural defenses. Even when it meant stopping early and lengthening the trip, she ordered us to pull up for the night when we found such defensible spots."

Chuckling, one of the rougher drivers said, "Three nights ago two riders hailed us and tried to come into our camp. Miss O'Shay warned them off. Told them we would kill the first man to approach the camp. They cussed us as unfriendly. We were not falling for that trick. They were going to scout out our camp for an attack."

With evident admiration, another driver spoke up, "Yep, the next night a group of fifteen came charging up yelling for us to lay our guns down. We had all spread out in the dark rather than laying in our beds. They saw no one in the camp but heard guns cock from every direction in the dark."

"Oh, they wanted us bad. They kept trying to get us to talk to reveal our positions. Finally, Miss O'Shay yelled, 'When the shooting starts, kill the talker first.'"

"They scattered so fast you would think a skunk sprayed them. The next day and night they followed us but never got the chance to hijack our supplies."

During this discussion, Tib sat looking completely unconcerned. At my arched eyebrows, Tib simply retorted, "That is why my dad sent me."

Contentedly full, the drivers laid down in the back of their now empty wagons and were soon asleep. Looking at her sleeping drivers, Tib turned to me and said, "It is late in the day, do you mind if we camp in the yard and depart in the morning?"

"Wise decision," said Kel.

I nodded and said, "The smaller stone house has a bedroom you can use."

"No thanks, I slept under a wagon on the trip up from Austin."

"It is no bother," I replied.

Indicating the discussion was over, Tib responded, "No," and walked out the door.

Darryl laughed and said, "Rye, you have a gift for getting under that woman's skin."

Nodding my head, I took their laughter in stride. I did have a knack for irritating Tib, the opposite of what I wanted to do. Sometimes no matter how hard you try, your socks just pick up sticker burrs.

• • •

Before the first hint of dawn, the drivers were up and preparing for their return to Austin. To my surprise, they were not hitching the mules to the wagons. They were saddling the mules.

Puzzled, I asked, "Aren't you taking the wagons back? We don't need five wagons."

Tib shook her head no. "One wagon was already yours and you bought the other four. Even if they were not yours, we could not take them back. If we tried, people might think we had gold in the wagons. No matter how cautious we might be, the odds are people would try to kill us to search the wagons. Better to leave the wagons here."

"Two of the mules are yours. Since we only rented you the other eight mules, we will need to buy two of your horses for mounts for two of the drivers."

The biggest mule driver, a hard man named Gebert, stepped forward and with trepidation said, "We will only need seven mules for the trip back."

Tib looked at him with a great deal of confusion and said, "There are ten of us, how can the ten of us get back with seven mounts?"

Looking at the ground the big man stammered, "Your father instructed me if the danger seemed too great and the ranch seemed defensible, two of us, Hobart and I, are to remain here with you until things settle down. He will send the Rangers down to get you."

While the giant of a man was talking, he appeared to grow smaller with every word. At the same time, Tib was puffing up, getting larger with each strangled breath.

Tib's face grew so red it looked like her freckles were fleeing. She hissed, "I am in charge and will not be told what to do."

Looking up from the ground, Gebert glanced at the other man assigned the dubious chore of remaining behind with Tib. Suddenly turning to the four cowboys, the frightened giant's eyes pleaded for help as he said, "Her dad said if we must, we are to tie Miss O'Shay up until the other drivers leave."

Tib's fists clenched and unclenched as she ground her teeth. Stopping just short of an eruption, Tib icily turned to me as though it was my fault and said with slow deliberation, "I will move into that empty room if you do not mind."

With that said, Tib yanked her belongings off the mule and stomped into the smaller stone house. From that point on, the smaller house was treated as though it was owned by Tib. Before entering, we would yell out requesting permission to stock the shelves with the new supplies and did so without ever seeing her.

The two mule drivers, Hobart and Gebert, were gentle giants tasked with ensuring we treated Tib respectfully. We encouraged the seven departing drivers to take extra horses to speed up their trip. At the journey's end, they were to place the horses for resale with Tib's father. We also encouraged them to leave us an extra team of mules, you never knew when we might have to pull another gold run with two wagons.

Taking extra horses would speed up the mule drivers' return, but more importantly, it would reduce the pressure on the grass around the homestead. Even with the departure of two Comanche ponies and six outlaw horses, we would still have fifteen horses and four mules.

•   •   •

Tib remained in her stone prison the entire morning. Kara was the one who induced her to come out. None of us men dared knock on Tib's bedroom door, but Kara incessantly banged away until Tib opened the door. When Tib flung the door open she glared out at chest height ready to tear into whoever dared disturb her. When Tib had to look down to see the small person banging on her door, her anger dissipated.

"Tell me a story about fairies," requested Kara.

"Um," Tib responded, taken aback by the request. Somewhat bewildered, Tib said, "Let's see if any of the others know a fairy story."

Walking hand in hand, the reluctant guest and the small child entered the bigger house. Without any indication she had pouted the morning away, Tib simply asked, "Does anyone know any fairy stories?"

Dennis who was sitting close to Heidi stepped up and without missing a beat, began one of his oft-repeated fairy stories. While retelling the story, the other men stood bug-eyed, unsure how to engage Tib.

"I need coffee," said Tib. Without waiting, she walked over and poured herself a cup as she listened to the story. After a half-dozen retellings of the same three fairy stories, Kara grabbed Tib's hand and took her outside to play with Kit.

Keeping an eye on the unlikely pair at play, I turned to Kel and asked, "When I met up with you in Austin it was evident something happened when you returned home, what was it?"

Kel replied, "The trip down was pretty uneventful. We kept to ourselves and did not draw too much attention, two men with two pack horses apiece is not unusual. Remember that huge pecan tree near the Brazos River where we collected those soft-shelled pecans each fall? We dug a hole at its base and buried the spare gold there."

"We dared not return home. Answering people's questions about the ranch would have tied us up for days. Even worse, kinfolk would have been angry if we refused to questions about the gold. Better to just avoid everyone."

"Upon our arrival, we each hired a friend and split up to pay folks for the land we bought. During the first day each time we paid off the land for twice what we originally promised, we were blessed as saints and saviors. By the second day, people heard we were paying off the land with gold at a higher price than agreed. Folks began to demand four times what we paid. Some even claimed they wanted their land voucher back and did not want to sell."

Darryl agreed, "Thanks to you, we had fake land vouchers. When they demanded more money or the voucher back, I would hold the gold in one hand and the voucher in the other. I would say, 'Makes no difference to me. Take which one you want, I got more places to visit before I head back west this afternoon.' They cussed me and took the gold. People are funny."

"Too many people always want more," sighed Kel. "Even the friends we hired. The last day the friend I hired told me the twenty dollars per day was not enough and he wanted one hundred dollars a day. This from a guy who had not earned ten dollars all year."

Kel continued, "When I sadly shook my head no, Bartlet drew a gun on me. I had to ram his horse with mine. After knocking Bartlet out, I left him on the side of the trail."

Darryl shook his head, "Almost the same thing happened to me. I knew Will ten years and had to beat his ass to leave."

Kel bowed his head and said, "I don't know what we were thinking, but we did not leave immediately. Considering the greedy folks trying to hold out the second day and our friends wanting more money, you would think we would have had the sense to hightail it back. Instead, Darryl and I stayed around another half-day selling the four Comanche ponies we used to pack the gold."

"We dickered for half a day and got less than one hundred dollars for the four ponies combined. Why did Darryl and I waste half a day for one hundred dollars when we arrived packing a hundred times that?"

Darryl picked up the story at this point. "That delay allowed some of Waller's less honorable citizens to gather and concoct a plan to rob us. After we sold the last pony Kel happened to see two fellows loitering down the trail. Through the woods, Kel saw another two who thought they were hidden."

"Well, you know Kel, he has hunted those woods and knows them like the back of his hand. Kel calmly walked his horse to the edge of the woods and once we got in there we took off. Those waiting for us did not know we had hit the spurs to our horses which gave us a good head start. Kel and I rode trails no one else knew. We count ourselves lucky to have made it back alive without killing anybody. No offense to you Dennis, I know you had to kill the two that attacked you."

CHAPTER TWENTY-THREE

Days passed and a pleasant routine developed. Just as the first rays of the sun would appear over the horizon I would gently knock on the outer door of the small stone house and enter. The knock was a courtesy and not intended to wake Tib. To my dismay, when opening the front door the hinges would wail as though in pain. Attempting to avoid waking Tib, I placed each foot down as quietly as possible on the wooden floor which screamed my presence with every step.

Passing through the house, I unbarred the door between the house and the barn. Stepping into the stone barn, the horses would nuzzle me, pulling at my sleeves as I unbarred the barn's outer door to the pasture. By the time I checked on each animal and shooed them into the pasture, Tib had risen and started boiling coffee.

Sitting next to the fire in the small house, a cup of hot coffee in our hands with no one else around was the sweetest moment of the day. Sipping the coffee seemed to melt the tension between the two of us. We would talk and each day it took us longer to finish that one cup of coffee before we joined Kel, Darryl, Dennis, Kara, Kit, Heidi, and the two mule drivers for breakfast in the big house.

Towards the end of the first week, Tib who was polite but distant from Heidi, asked where she slept. When I pointed to the loft where Dennis slept, Tib's eyes narrowed, and she radiated disapproval. Tib's disapproval of Heidi was unfair, but I had no right to tell Tib the story behind Heidi's attachment to Dennis.

When we finished our coffee, a stern-faced Tib stalked into the house, grasped Heidi by the hand, and pulled the bewildered girl down to the creek. A much different Tib returned. Tear streaks lined Tib's cheeks, and she held Heidi's hand like a beloved sister.

The next morning during our shared coffee cup Tib told me what happened. "I took Heidi down to the creek. In a patronizing voice, I explained how inappropriate it was for a young lady to be sleeping with a man she was not married to and it needed to stop immediately."

"With a sad smile, Heidi explained that she watched the Comanche kill her entire family. When she tried to escape the first day of her captivity the Comanche took all her clothes. Riding for a week with no clothes her skin burned, blistered, and roasted to the point she has permanent splotches like Darryl's Appaloosa. When Dennis found her, her skin was so ruined she had to remain naked for a week around Dennis, Kel, and you. Three times a day Dennis helped bathe her and rubbed a healing poultice over every single intimate inch of her body. She can only sleep at night if she can touch Dennis' foot or hand, curled up, away from, but touching him."

Remorse all over her face, Tib continued, "I burst into tears. Sobbing I told Heidi I was so sorry for judging her. I invited her to come to Austin and live with me, but Heidi said she only feels safe in the stone castle with you cowboys."

• • •

Like clockwork, the hawks began their February migration north through Lost Maples. This was my third time to experience their migration and I was again struck by the number and types of hawks flying overhead. Witnessing these usually solitary birds joining a river of their kin flowing north was different this time. Sharing the awe of thousands of migrating hawks with Tib felt as though I was seeing the wonder of their flight for the first time.

While they lived with us, we hired the two mule drivers to help us patrol and mark our boundaries. Two adults remained behind to protect the house while the other five stacked rock marking the new one hundred and fifty thousand acres we had purchased during the last trip to Austin. Inevitably while stacking rock and just monitoring our property, we encountered people on our land. One of us would approach them while the others kept their hands close to their guns. We would politely pull out our map and show them they were trespassing. Most complained but moved. Those trespassers who refused, moved at the point of our guns.

We were grateful we did not have to shoot anyone. However, we knew it was just a matter of time before a shooting occurred. Encampments outside of our canyon brimmed with growing frustration. People had left their homes and farms after hearing stories of our gold strike and had pinned their hopes on easy riches. Days and then weeks went by with no gold strikes as disgruntled people abandoned their camps.

The good people who failed to find gold returned home. Those citizens who remained behind began to covet our gold. When we worked on the boundaries, one person always had a cocked rifle in their hands.

Over time it got so we could not work on the rock walls without someone taking a pot shot at us. Eventually, we gave up working on the boundary. We figured when things calmed down we would go back to building the markers. Reluctantly we retreated to the house and sat back waiting for the inevitable.

Resigned, we knew it was just a matter of time before people decided the only way to get gold was to take ours. We saw a rider or two down by the mine, but Kel and his marksmanship scared them off.

For a while, nothing happened. I think the gold seekers thought we would load a wagon with gold and foolishly try to drive for Austin. When it became evident we were hunkered down, they tried to feel out our defenses.

Their probes began with single riders who would hail the house and ask if they could come in for a cup of coffee. A carefully placed bullet in front of their horses let them know that ploy would not work. Once a group of five men pulled up and said they were Rangers hunting a wanted man and needed to search our home. When they were unable to present badges, Kel filled a Spanish blunderbuss with rock salt. He fired both barrels sending them smartly on their way.

We tried to keep the pressure down on the pasture next to the barn by setting some of the horses free to roam as we had done in the past. The first night the Comanche ponies did not come back. We suspected the outlaws had grabbed them while out grazing.

Unfortunately, we did not have a choice and the next day let loose the four outlaw horses. The outlaw horses did not return either.

Even though the herd was reduced to six horses and four mules, the pasture was overgrazed and offered little to eat. We turned the four mules and two horses loose. When the animals failed to return that evening no one was surprised. The outlaws' stolen herd was expanding.

During the night, the four remaining horses were kept in the stone barn where they were allowed the merest hint of hay. Releasing the horses into the fenced pasture where they nibbled at what little remained of the once luxurious pasture kept them alive. Down to our last four horses, we knew protecting the animals was important. We took turns covering the pasture from the house's rifle ports.

Four days later a group of ten horsemen rushed the pasture. I think they hoped we would run from the house to protect the horses. What they did not know was that the rifle ports in both houses were laid out such that from their corners, Kel and Dennis could cover the front of the house and the horse pasture. The other two corners covered all approaches to the back of both houses.

Weapons filled each of our corners. Over time, we bought and traded until we had collected our preferred weapons, usually of the same caliber to simplify ammunition needs. None of us wasted our time with Brown Bess muskets. All of us had at least two of the percussion-cap Kentucky long rifles. I had two of the carbine versions of the .75 caliber Baker Rifle, their shorter barrels made for easier transportation since I spent so much of my time on a horse. Likewise, Dennis and Darryl each had two .40 caliber Hawken or plains rifles whose shorter barrels were their rifle of choice when on a horse. Kel represented his family well with four Kentucky long rifles, four Baker Rifles, and a half-dozen other rifles he used depending on the occasion.

We each had two Colt Patersons. In a day and age when the vast majority of guns were single-shot, our eight five-shot Patersons presented a formidable front.

Kel of course had a dozen various pistols. Some of his pistols were tiny and disappeared in your hand. Others looked like they were rifles with the barrels sawed off.

The outlaws did not know it, but they were at a distinct disadvantage with their single-shot weapons. They would be rushing four men who each had at least four single-shot rifles and at least two five-shot Patersons. Tib, Heidi, and the two mule drivers would be reloading as we fired.

When ten outlaws broke from cover to rush the pasture, Kel killed one at two hundred yards while Dennis wisely held his fire. Reaching for a new rifle, at one hundred and fifty yards Kel must have hurried his shot because he missed. Dropping the rifle, at one hundred yards Kel knocked a rider out of his saddle while Dennis, unfortunately, shot a horse. Quickly dropping their spent rifles, Kel and Dennis both dropped outlaws at fifty yards.

The six surviving outlaws turned tail and headed for cover. They had come to kill us so there was no mercy in Kel or Dennis. With their next four shots, Kel and Dennis each killed an attacker as the other four survivors retreated.

While ten outlaws were attacking from the pasture to the right of the house, fifteen outlaws assaulted the house from the rear. Darryl and I did not possess Kel's sharpshooting skills. We waited until they were one hundred yards from the house before we shot. Neither Darryl nor I looked to see if we hit anything as we grabbed a new set of rifles, but when we looked up neither of us had hit our targets. Taking our time, at seventy-five yards one of us emptied a saddle. At fifty yards I missed, and Darryl found his target. At twenty-five yards, we both scored hits.

Four riderless horses galloped around outside as the remaining eleven outlaws came close enough to pose a danger to us in the rifle ports. We leaned back away from the opening as several shots ricocheted off the narrow openings.

Half the outlaws jumped off their horses and ran to the front door. I do not know what they were thinking, perhaps hoping we had a flimsy door. When the outlaws banged into the door I think they were shocked the door did not give an inch. Since we had allowed no strangers into the house, they had no idea the door was solid oak and double-barred.

After firing from the rifle ports with their single-shot rifles, Kel and Dennis leaned almost straight down to empty their Patersons at the men congregated at the front door. The outlaws thought getting to the door meant they were close to overwhelming us. Little did they know it meant entering a killing field. The five men closest to the door became an unmoving mound of bloody flesh. Scattering away from the door, the six remaining outlaws spurred their horses away from the house.

Like Kel and Dennis, we saw those six men riding away as people who wanted to kill people we loved. Tib and one of the mule drivers had been busy reloading our rifles. Taking our time, Darryl, and I each fired four times and took out two of the retreating outlaws. Only four of the eleven escaped.

Kara suddenly grabbed me and pointed to the hill behind the house. Four men were busy setting fire to brush and rolling it down the hill. I yelled, "Kel, they are back of the house."

Firing rapidly, we took out the four men, two falling in the burning brush they were trying to roll down the hill. Fortunately for us, unknown to them, our stone house was not going to burn.

Quiet suddenly descended on us. For the first time, we noticed the black cloud of gun smoke inside the house and the heavy smell of burnt powder in the air. When the fight started, we had no problem picking out targets. Now that the fight was over, everything was obscured by low-lying clouds of black gun powder smoke.

The silence was broken by moans from wounded outlaws. Until visibility improved, no one was leaving the safety of the house. In ten minutes the smoke cleared, and we could see the carnage.

There were twenty-one bodies spread out from as far away as two hundred and fifty yards to a pile at the front door. Several were moaning, but we were in no hurry to go out there and risk getting shot. One kept moaning like he was in terrible pain. We were not falling for that old trick. There were at least a dozen outlaws still out there ready for an opportunity to kill us.

Ten minutes with the moaning weakening, I yelled out, "If someone wants to get your man, you can."

Suddenly a rifle shot rang out from where the outlaws were hiding. You could hear the thud as the bullet hit the moaning man who suddenly lay still.

"That is a hard man out there," Dennis commented.

Following Dennis's comment, we all looked at him and for the first time realized Dennis was wounded. Blood ran in a zig-zag line from the top of Dennis' head, down the side of his face and neck where it pooled at his collar.

Heidi ran over and thrust her hands through Dennis's hair. Clutching his hair, Heidi's shoulders began to heave, and she suddenly burst into laughter.

We were all rooted to the spot, unsure what to do. The laughter just seemed so, well, inappropriate.

Holding up one hand as though to stop anyone from approaching, Heidi said, "Sorry, the laughter was out of relief. A bullet must have hit the rifle port causing a piece of limestone to break loose and cut Dennis' scalp. He is fine, nothing a little soap and water won't cure."

Dennis looked around at everyone. "Why am I the only one who ever gets wounded? An arrow through my arm and now a bleeder on my head."

CHAPTER TWENTY-FOUR

Sitting behind our safe walls awaiting the next attack, we watched the sun rise as familiar sounds broke the morning silence. Quacks and honks indicated ducks and geese were migrating again. The peaceful honks of geese traveling north felt out of place with people waiting to kill us.

During the third day of the siege, the sounds of a terrible battle began to rage in the distance. The distinct pop of rifles, pistols, and shotguns echoed off the canyon walls. On cue, the barrage of shots suddenly stopped. With the echo of the last shot fading, an eerie quiet settled throughout the canyon. After an hour, four men rode toward the house their hands raised in the air long before they came into rifle range.

"Hello, the house," the lead rider yelled. "Captain Eldridge sent us down to help you."

None of us were too trusting after our experiences during the last two months. "Don't know that I believe you," I yelled.

One rider proceeded forward, his hands still in the air. When he drew near enough to make out his face, I recognized the beanpole Ranger that Captain Eldridge had assigned to guard my wagon. Sam pointed at the direction from which they had ridden and said, "Those boys won't bother you anymore."

I yelled down, "Sam, I am glad to see you. You boys can set your horses free in the pasture and leave your tack on the railing."

The Rangers set their horses loose and squared away their gear. Walking into the stone house they commented on and admired its defenses. One said, "Stone takes longer to build, but it doesn't burn like timber." A second one commented, "Course sod houses don't burn much." A third added, "Stone stops bullets a lot better than sod or wood."

Pointing towards the yard, the Rangers said, "Got yourself quite a few ripe bodies out there."

Nonchalantly, Dennis said, "Yep, for the past three days the neighbors have objected to us planting them."

Our newfound friends sat down and began to sip their coffee as we expectantly waited for them to describe what just happened. Like most Texans, these young Rangers loved telling a story almost as much as they enjoyed delaying a story to build up suspense.

A lanky Ranger turned to Tib and said, "Your father will be glad to see you are alive."

Sam shook his head, "When you boys deposited all that gold you set the rooster loose. Every outlaw within five hundred miles rode as quickly as possible to Austin. I believe they were afraid the banks would be empty before they got a chance to steal their share."

"Captain Eldridge figured it was an opportunity for the Republic of Texas to thin its outlaw population. He recalled two dozen Rangers from border duty and put three Rangers in each of the four banks where you deposited gold."

"We had a bank robbery attempt four times the first week, three times the second week, and two attempts a week for the next month. Twenty-six bank robbers were killed and another six were captured. Some escaped, but I would not be surprised if they died later because no one got away with less than one serious wound."

"Just about the time the bank robberies were tapering off, Tib's dad came to Captain Eldridge. Mr. O'Shay figured it would take two and half weeks to get those heavy wagons to Lost Maples and another two weeks to get back. The wagons were only a week late, but your dad was worried. Captain Eldridge sympathized, but the bank robberies were still occurring, and he needed to keep thinning out the outlaws while the opportunity existed. The Captain promised if you had not returned in another week, he would send the Rangers after you."

"A week later Captain Eldridge sent us four to look for you. We found your men two days from Lost Maples. Looked like they had been ambushed two weeks ago. A thorough search revealed seven bodies and we knew there were ten of you."

Tib burst into tears and buried her face in her hands. I got up and awkwardly put my hand on her shoulder. Tib looked up at me and placed her hand on top of mine as she continued to silently weep for the murdered drivers.

"We buried the drivers and trailed the killers. The trail was several weeks old, but there were over thirty horses and a half-dozen mules, so the trail was easy to track. We trailed them to their encampment a half-mile from here."

"After what those killers did to your men, and at the time we thought maybe you Miss O'Shay, we were not in a forgiving mood. We rode in shooting. No one was allowed to escape. We rode down anyone who survived our two passes through the camp. Looks like there were originally thirty or forty of them, there were only fourteen when we found them. From the bodies in the yard, I can see where the others ended up."

The Ranger finished up by saying, "The Republic of Texas thanks you for eliminating the outlaws in the yard and pasture. You are entitled to their horses as well as their guns."

Sam continued, "The capital is too far and there are too many for us to haul these bodies back to Austin for identification. Do you have anybody who could draw their faces? We can send out posters indicating they are no longer wanted. I suspect there are rewards for the twenty-one y'all shot."

I stood up and shook each of their hands, "You saved our bacon when you rolled through their camp. Tell Captain Eldridge to put the rewards in the same Ranger fund as the others."

Kel spoke up, "What should we do with all these bodies? I believe in burying, but thirty-five graves is a lot of digging."

Sam nodded, "We will help you. The bodies can be rolled into a crevice, packed with wood, and burned. After the fire burns out we can roll rocks and dirt on top of whatever remains."

Though I had insisted on the burial of the Karankawa, Comanche, and outlaws in the past, I did not have it in me to insist on thirty-five graves this time. We hooked the mules to a wagon and hauled the bodies to a deep crevice a mile away.

We stripped the bodies of their weapons and ammunition. Checking their pockets for letters or other items of identification, we found the same thing in all their pockets, five twenty-dollar gold pieces.

I turned to Sam, "With little to no notice, someone was able to give these thirty-five men and four others, a hundred dollars each in gold. Who keeps four thousand dollars in gold coins readily available?"

Sam looked at me, "Gives one pause. I will turn over the gold to Captain Eldridge, I bet he has a suspicion on the gold's origins."

Like so much firewood, we alternated layers of bodies and layers of wood. The pile was slow to burn initially, but once lit, to my surprise the fire burned hot.

Seeing my surprise, a Ranger the size of a small mountain said, "Such fires burn hot because of all the fat in the body."

I turned away from the fire and went to collect more firewood. Dennis came along. Leaning in, Dennis whispered, "Do you know who you were talking just to?"

"Uh no."

Beaming, Dennis said, "That six foot two and two-hundred-and-forty-pound mass of muscle is Big Foot Wallace."[1]

I could not help but grin. Dennis and I looked at each other. Though full-grown men, we giggled like children. Everyone had heard of Big Foot Wallace. He was a hero. When his brother and cousin were killed at Goliad, Big Foot Wallace left Virginia and vowed to make the Mexicans pay, and he did.

Dennis said, "Try not to be obvious when you turn around, but that fella Sam keeps deferring to is Lieutenant Ben McCulloch. I don't know what he is doing here. He was elected to the Republic of Texas House of Representatives in 1839 and should be sitting in Austin."[2]

Admonishing me, Dennis continued, "Now that you know who they are, don't go getting all tongue-tied and act the fool around them."

Glancing in wonder at my companions, we tended the fire through the night, tossing in additional firewood as the blaze burned down. Burning the bodies was not enough, the fire needed to keep roaring to burn the bones. We had no desire in the weeks and months ahead to come across some animal gnawing on a human arm or leg bone.

While feeding the fire it was important to watch for floating embers. Having fought for our land, we did not want to set the canyon ablaze.

When the sun rose on the horizon, the fire had burned down, and we could see that even the bones had burned to ash. Returning to the house, we discovered several pots of coffee gurgling and breakfast almost ready.

Sitting around the table piled with plates of bacon and biscuits, one of the Rangers mentioned in a melancholy voice he wished Deaf Smith was with them when they taught those outlaws a lesson. Hearing his old friend's name, Kel spoke up, "He was the bravest man I ever knew. I was sad to hear he passed away in 1837."[3]

While they ate, the Rangers began to regale each other with stories that got more outrageous with each telling. Licking their fingers after finishing up the last of the bacon, the Rangers asked permission to sleep for several hours before they returned to Austin.

With the sun was directly overhead, the Rangers began to wake up from their three-hour slumber. Working efficiently, the Rangers caught their horses and packed their gear.

Of the thirty-five outlaw horses, several had been killed during the gun battles and several had run away. Twenty-eight horses had been rounded up, of which we were entitled to fourteen. We already had too many horses but took the fourteen intending to take the horses to San Antonio and trade them for several high-quality Spanish mares. The Rangers agreed to take Mr. O'Shay's six mules back with them.

Glancing over my shoulder I caught sight of Tib exiting the stone house with a bag. My heart froze. The thought never occurred to me that the arrival of the Rangers signaled Tib's departure. I stumbled over to her with a stricken look on my face, unable to find any words. Tib nodded and saddled up one of the outlaw's horses. She tossed her leg over the side and looked down at me with a face absent of clues.

Heidi came out of the house and the two women hugged each other with the passion of sisters. The harsh frontier forged many such bonds between people.

Tib's eyes moved from my face to the house. I saw a sad smile grace her face as I followed her eyes. Turning I saw Tib was watching Kara approach.

Her head barely reaching the bottom of the stir-up, Kara held her hands out and commanded, "Up."

Bending down, I lifted Kara, and Tib gave Kara the hug I wished I was receiving. Lowering Kara I glanced up to see Tib staring intently at my face. With a sinking feeling, I stalked away, feeling a sadness I had not known since my father's death. I did not watch Tib ride away. Instead, I stumbled to the pasture and talked to Woe.

Darryl walked over and listened to my conversation with Woe. Five minutes passed before he offered, "You should have said something to Tib."

"What could I have said?"

"Oh, how about please stay."

"Tib was not going to stay on an isolated ranch with four strange men."

"You might be right Rye. But you don't know until you ask." With that statement, Darryl turned and walked to the house.

That night the quiet within the house was deafening. We had lived with danger and in harmony with Tib. No one missed the danger, but we missed Tib. More specifically, I missed Tib.

The next morning, the sprinkling of early blooming bluebonnets in the pasture and meadows had erupted overnight into a carpet of blue. With Tib gone, the flowers that produced so much excitement last year, no longer stirred my soul.

To Kara's delight, the butterfly migration began, but their beauty made me sad. Tiny hummingbirds appeared for their migration north but the magic they used to instill was gone. All around me, the world was bursting with the vitality of spring, but to me, the world was grey.

In the following weeks, we had no more trouble. Since no one found even a trace of gold, the last of the would-be miners admitted defeat. There were no more attempts to take our gold. The outlaws were dead and as Captain Eldridge would say, "A sizeable dent had been made in the outlaw population of Texas."

Every couple of days a Ranger would stop by for a meal or a place to bed down for the night. One day Ranger Benjamin Franklin Highsmith stopped by to drop off some choice cuts of buffalo he had shot fifteen miles south on Little Creek.[4] Word spread we were under the protection of the Rangers and people left us alone.

With times a little safer, during hunting trips each of us would drop by the cave where Kit was born and drop off bags of gold. Having a cache of gold away from the homestead seemed important.

NOTES

1. *Handbook of Texas Online*, J. Frank Dobie, "Wallace, William Anderson (Big Foot)," accessed May 7, 2020, https://www.tshaonline.org/handbook/online/articles/fwa36. Big Foot Wallace (1817-1899) carried himself like his Highlander predecessors William Wallace and Robert Bruce. He was a friend to Bowie and Travis and served in every noteworthy battle. A member of the failed Mier Expedition, Big Foot was incarcerated in and survived the infamous Mexican Perote Prison. Big Foot went on to serve as a Captain in the Texas Rangers and commanded his own company of Rangers.

2. *Handbook of Texas Online*, Thomas W. Cutrer, "McCullough, Benjamin," accessed May 7, 2020, https://www.tshaonline.org/handbook/online/articles/fmc34. Ben McCullough (1811-1862) who was friends with Davey Crockett, agreed to leave Tennessee and follow Crocket to the Alamo. Ben was unable to catch up with Crockett after contracting measles, but he did fight at San Jacinto. General Houston was so impressed with Ben's command of one of the Twin Sisters at the battle of San Jacinto he gave him a battlefield promotion to Lieutenant. Ben served in almost every major battle from 1836 to 1845.

3. *Handbook of Texas Online*, Thomas W. Cutrer, "Smith, Erastus (Deaf)" accessed May 7, 2020, https://www.tshaonline.org/handbook/online/articles/fsm10. Deaf Smith (1787-1837) settled in Texas in 1821. Despite losing his hearing as a child, Deaf Smith was involved in the Battle of Conception, Grass Fight, Siege of Bexar, carried Travis' February 15, 1836 letter from the Alamo, Battle of San Jacinto, and commanded a company of Rangers.

4. Walton, *Bear Meat 'n' Honey*, 12. Ben Highsmith (1817-1905) is reported to have shot a buffalo in the early 1840s under a pecan

tree fifteen miles south of Lost Maples on Little Creek. This story is shared by his granddaughter Oma Highsmith Jones Lewis who was born in 1903 several miles south of Lost Maples. Oma's grandfather Ben Highsmith came to Texas in 1823. She remembers the family repeating stories Grandpa Highsmith shared about the Alamo and his friends Bowie, Crockett, McCulloch, Travis, and Austin. Ben fought at Velasco, Brushy Creek, Plum Creek, Nueces Canyon, Enchanted Rock, Bandera Pass, Salado Creek, Hondo Creek, Resaca de la Palmas, Monterey, and Buena Vista. Ben carried Travis's last letter (February 18, 1836) to Fannin. By the time Ben returned to the Alamo, it was surrounded and from a distance, he had to watch it fall.

CHAPTER TWENTY-FIVE

Days went by, then weeks, as we adjusted to Tib's absence and began to focus on marking our boundaries. We spent a painful soul-numbing month building rock cairns to mark our land. Toward the end of April, we were approached by a thin man on an equally skinny burro who introduced himself as Juan. With Darryl translating, the man said, "I lived in these canyons before the Revolution and fled to Mexico after the war. Mexico is now as dangerous for my family as Texas. Is there work or a place where we might live without being bothered?"

We were sick to death of building rock boundaries and here was a man looking for work. Without hesitation, an agreement was quickly reached to hire Juan. We invited our new wall builder to come down to the house and camp. Rather than being happy at the opportunity to camp with us, the suggestion caused Juan alarm. Politely, but firmly he insisted on camping near his work. Shrugging we pointed out the boundary, indicating we would be back in several days.

Returning with supplies two days later we caught Juan off guard and his alarm was visible. When we first met, Juan was not sure if he could trust us, and had hidden his family while we talked.

We rode up to discover in addition to a thin wife, Juan had a small daughter Kara's age, a son that must have been twelve or thirteen, and a daughter who looked to be seventeen. Like the others, the older daughter was thin and worn out, but possessed a beauty that even starvation and constant worry could not hide.

Juan quickly hid his children. How could he know whether we were evil men?

With Darryl translating, Kel informed Juan, "We are leaving you coffee, flour, sugar, and some other necessities as part of your wages. You can obtain more at the house any time you want."

Turning our horses to go, Darryl told Juan, "Our daughter Kara is your youngest daughter's age if she ever wants to visit."

The next day Kel returned to the camp with a great deal more food. Kel went alone, and we did not find out what he had done until the next day. When questioned Kel said, "Did you see how skinny those kids were. I just don't cotton to the idea that family is up there in the rocks starving when we have so much food."

Before the sun rose the next day, Kel commented that he was going hunting. When he came back that evening, Kel did so without any game. We spent the evening joshing Kel that he was getting heavy-footed and had lost his ability to hunt. After several hours of ribbing, Kel uncharacteristically exploded and said, "I shot a big doe and gave it to the family."

The room was silent. What was going on? Kel had been to that camp three out of the last five days. Darryl being more familiar with women than us said, "It's that girl."

Uncharacteristic for Kel, he turned and glared at Darryl. Then it dawned on us, Kel had gone soft over the scrawny girl up in the hills. Kel was not the kind of guy who chased girls, so we knew this was serious. Whether Kel liked it or not, we were determined to help him.

The next day without Kel knowing, Darryl and I headed up to Juan's camp. The family seemed much less alarmed with our visit than the first time. We stepped off our horses and in broken Spanish I looked directly at Juan and said, "The rock boundary is needed, but the more important task is the care of our horse herd which had grown beyond our ability. Do you know anything about horses?"

Juan's eyes lit up. The fear usually hovering in Juan's eyes was replaced with excitement as he smiled and vigorously nodded yes.

Darryl said, "We have twenty-nine horses and four mules. They need to be rotated among the various places where grass grows in the canyon. Would you and your son be interested in such a job?"

You could almost feel the energy crackling from Juan as he vigorously shook his head yes. Darryl smiled and said, "It would be important for you and your family to move down near the house where we pasture and house the livestock."

I could see worry cross Juan's face, so Darryl translated as I said, "We are good men who will not harm your family. By living close, we can protect your family from Indians and bad white men."

Juan seemed to weigh the words carefully, then nodded yes. We helped the family pack their meager belongings and loaded the children on the horses as the adults walked.

When we approached the house, Dennis and Kel stood in the doorway bewildered. I explained what was happening and for goodness sake, Kel practically glowed. Out of the corner of my eye, I noticed that the daughter Consuela did not seem displeased either. One did not need Irish blood to see something had already ignited between the two.

To the little family, I explained we had a pet cougar that they must not harm. This information was poorly received, and the family's terror was such that I thought they were about to turn tail and run for the hills. At that moment Kara exited the door pulling Kit by the ears. Kara stopped and stared intently at the family's three-year-old, Teresa. Smiling broadly, Kara rushed forward, took Teresa's hand, and started jabbering away in a manner she had never done with us. The two began a long conversation that for all practical purposes, did not contain a single shared word from their different languages.

Dennis introduced Heidi to Juan and his family. They quickly accepted Heidi, never needing an explanation about her role. Juan and the women in his family knew only too well the challenges in living on the Texas frontier. A woman had to make her way as best as she could.

Juan refused to move into either stone house, so we offered to help him build his own home fifty feet from the main house. Kel practically worked himself to death helping erect Juan's dwelling. Though they never said a word to or looked directly at each other, Kel and Consuela were always within twenty feet of one another.

While working on the stone house Juan began to open up and shared some of his family's history and knowledge of Lost Maples. With Darryl translating, Juan said, "The Spanish originally called this canyon, the Canon del Solidad, the Canyon of Solitude.[1] But there was no solitude, for hundreds of years this was Apache land."

Juan said, "Apache graves can be found as far as five miles north, fifteen miles south, and several miles east and west of your canyon.[2] Some of the dead are buried in caves and others on top of the flat parts of mountains north of here.[3] Beware of any large mound that looks out of place, it is probably an Apache burial mound."

"The Apache considered flint sacred. They had two mines, one near where Mill Creek and the Sabinal River meet, and another not far from Gabriel Hole.[4] The other canyon to the west where the maples grow was also considered a sacred place by the Indians."[5]

Pointing to one of our canyons, Juan said, "Up there on the canyon walls grows a tree that is often just a large bush that produces the berries you call mulberries. The Apache often made their bows from the mulberry tree.[6] On the edge of the woods, there peeks out a small tree with white flowers you call the dogwood, the Apache made their arrow shafts from the dogwood."[7]

Kel asked, "How is it you know so much about the Apache?"

With pride, Juan said, "Such information has been handed down for generations in my family. Long ago my great grandfather was captured as a child by the Apache. He was raised by them for ten years before the Spanish bought his freedom. My ancestor did not want to return to the Spanish. With the Apache, men sit around the fire and talk, hunt, and raid. Men are treated as slaves by the Spanish. My ancestor, he did not want to leave the Apache, but the Spanish insisted."

"After living with the Spanish several years my great grandfather slipped away one night and returned to this canyon. The Apache remembered him and allowed him to pick an Apache wife. My family lived in peace in the canyon for many years."

Kel asked, "Why did the Apache leave such a beautiful country?"

Juan shivered, "Comanche. The Apache were fierce. But the Comanche, they were like the wall of water that washes down the canyon after heavy rain. More than a hundred years ago the Comanche with their massive horse herds moved into what you call the panhandle. For years, the constant Comanche raids pushed and pushed the Apache. Gradually the Apache found themselves forced south and west of Texas."

• • •

The day Juan's house was completed, Kel immediately began to build another between Juan's house and the big stone house. He refused to answer any questions about the house and refused all assistance in building it.

Consuela watched Kel's work on the house and inspected his progress when he was not around. On several occasions Consuela casually remarked about some aspect of the house and Kel would rip out and revise his previous work.

When the second house was finished, Kel shocked everyone by asking Juan for his daughter's hand in marriage. The proposal was no surprise to Consuela who immediately said yes.

Water was thrown on everything when Juan stated they were Catholic and demanded they find a priest to conduct the ceremony. Kel wanted to be married and married immediately.

Since Darryl was the one who spoke Spanish without sounding like a buffoon, it was agreed he and Kel would go in search of a priest. Juan suggested they go to San Antonio which was a three-day ride southeast. The more we thought about it, this seemed like a good opportunity to trade our excess horses for some good Spanish mares.

After a long-drawn-out discussion in which Juan continuously consulted with his wife, Juan eventually agreed to accompany us to San Antonio where he knew some horse merchants. Juan was reluctant to leave his family alone. He finally consented when Dennis and Heidi pledged their lives to protect Juan's family.

With myself, Darryl, Kel, Juan, and Juan's son Javier, we departed Lost Maples with a herd of twenty horses for San Antonio. We decided to keep two of the tough little Comanche ponies, Woe, Darryl's Appaloosa and the paint, the chestnut mare, Kel's Grulla and his blood bay, Dennis' sorrel, and the sealskin bay.

Taking our time to avoid stressing or injuring any of the horses, we made it to San Antonio in four and a half days. Our first order of business was to dispose of the horse herd. Boarding and feeding that many horses would be expensive and since we were strangers in town, there was always the chance our horses might start disappearing.

Juan quickly located a horse trader he trusted, and the dance began. We asked to see the Spanish mares the trader possessed, and he asked to examine our horses. He gushed over the quality of his horses and wept when discussing the many shortcomings of the horses we proposed to trade. While Juan and I wrangled with the horse trader, Kel and Darryl went in search of a priest.

Four hours of haggling later, we traded our twenty horses for three magnificent Spanish mares that reeked of nobility. Tears ran down the trader's cheeks as he said goodbye to the mares. Sobbing he contended that if his cousin had not married the niece of Juan's maternal grandfather from his uncle's side, no such theft from him would have been permitted.

In fairness, we gave up not only quantity but quality. If we were better organized for raising horses, I would have kept ten of the horses we traded away. We just did not have sufficient fenced pasture with water sources developed yet. Some day we would.

A disappointed Darryl and Kel joined us. Kel had managed to buy two wedding rings, a wedding dress, and a variety of women's garments that he was assured would make for a happy wife. Despite their best efforts, they could not find a priest willing to ride to Lost Maples. Every priest insisted the couple come to San Antonio.

Juan was adamant, no priest, no marriage. Somberly, Kel took one of the spare horses and told us to meet him by the Guadalupe River at the edge of town.

Kel rode up an hour later pulling the reins of the blood bay on which rode a priest with his mouth gagged and his hands tied behind his back. In desperation, Kel had kidnapped a priest.

We rode like hell before a posse could be gathered to give chase. Three days later we rode into Lost Maples with a very unhappy man of the cloth.

The following day, Consuela stood decked out in white, as Kel wore a black suit that cost more than any horse he had ever owned. The priest was absent, and I went in search of him. I found Darryl and the obstinate priest in our little Indian graveyard. I could only understand every fourth word, but I did understand the tone of the words.

Darryl later repeated to me the conversation he had with the stubborn priest. "This is where we bury people who upset us. Can you count the number of graves here? You will marry that couple and give them your blessing, or I will bury a piece of you in the graves of each of these Comanche warriors. You can spend the afterlife being chased by heathens."

The ceremony was a success. To a cheering audience, Kel carried Consuela over the threshold of the home that she had ever so casually supervised during its construction.

NOTES

1. Walton, *Bear Meat 'n' Honey*, 133. The Sabinal Canyon was originally an Apache stronghold and contained several Apache villages. The Apache used the canyon as their base for raiding Spanish settlements like San Antonio. As the Comanche swept deeper into Texas they pushed out the Apache and the Comanche used the canyon as a path south for raiding.

2. Ibid., 60-62, 172.

3. Ibid., 81.

4. Ibid., 60-62.

5. Ibid., 86. Currently named Mystic Canyon.

6. Turner, *Remarkable Plants of Texas*, 53.

7. Ibid., 22.

CHAPTER TWENTY-SIX

The next morning the priest was up early. Disapproval reeked from his stern face despite the bag slung over his shoulder overflowing with items from the storehouse. The agitated priest was saying something with great volume in Spanish and impatiently pointing toward San Antonio.

Dennis fiddled with his gear as we saddled our horses. Finally, I said, "Dammit Dennis, have you forgotten how to saddle a horse?"

Hunching his shoulders, Dennis said, "We have a preacher. What would you think if I asked Heidi to marry me?"

I clasped Dennis in a bear hug and said, "That would be the smartest thing you ever did, that girl loves you."

"Does she love me or the guy who rescued her from the Comanche?"

"Dennis, you cannot separate the two. You are, who you are, and the cowboy who saved her. Your gentleness and the fact you never judged her is how you won Heidi."

"Go now, ask her before this belligerent priest runs off."

Looking over his shoulder, Dennis saw Heidi in the door watching him pack. She did not like to be apart from Dennis and never slept while he was away.

Dennis took her by the hand and walked down to the dam at the bottom of the pasture. "Heidi, I uh, we have a priest here. Think hard before you answer. I uh, want to spend my life with you."

"I rescued you, but anyone could have been the one. Kel, Darryl, or Rye could have walked up to that bush. I want you to marry me because you love me, not just because by some luck I found you."

Heidi squared her shoulders. "I am lucky you found me. You saved my life."

Tears appeared in her eyes and then poured in streams down her cheeks as Heidi seemed to crumble inward. "It would not be right for you to marry me. I could never be a decent wife for you. I never told you. But, every night, those Comanche bucks had their way with me."

Dennis bowed his head and then looked Heidi directly in the eyes. "Oh Heidi, I would give anything to have kept all those awful things from happening to you. None of that matters. I love you. I cannot even imagine my life before I met you. Will you marry me?"

Matching Dennis's direct gaze, Heidi lowered her head and sobbed, "Yes."

Holding Heidi's hand tightly they walked back into the house. Waking up Darryl, Dennis said, "Tell that priest to hold his horses, he has another wedding to perform."

I roused everyone out of bed, and we watched as Dennis and Heidi married. Turning to Darryl I said, "You might want to unsaddle Dennis's horse, he has a honeymoon to celebrate. While you are at it, saddle your horse, you are going to San Antonio with me."

●   ●   ●

Kel and Darryl were happy, but I was not. I missed Tib. We made several trips to San Antonio which was sixty-five miles closer than Austin and had everything we needed. San Antonio had everything, except Tib.

We had not experienced any outlaw visits since the Ranger shoot-out and decided to risk a trip to Austin so Dennis could sign all the bank documents. Heidi was not happy to be left alone. She demanded to come along, but Dennis who always indulged her, refused because we were not sure if traveling was safe.

Dennis, Darryl, and I would ride to Austin and Kel would remain at the ranch. Kel smiled and offered no arguments about missing out on the trip. Since we were kids and young bucks, Kel never looked twice at females. Kel falling so quickly and hard for someone was a shock to us all. Yet here was Kel, standing on his front porch with his arm around his wife watching us prepare to depart.

Packing our gear, I expected Kara to cling to us and beg us to stay or take her with us. Instead, she and Juan's daughter Teresa happily played in front of the house. Strange women had taken my best friend, cousin, and daughter. Well, I guess that is the way of the world.

Handshakes, hugs, and goodbyes were exchanged. No one said it, but Darryl, Dennis, and I were glad to be off the ranch. Remaining on the ranch first for building and then safety reasons had begun to wear on us. There was a giddiness among the three of us, excited to be anywhere but where we were.

Though Austin was northeast, we planned to ride south for a day to more closely exam the pastureland we had purchased in our last trip to Austin and to examine potential purchases in the future. That entire first day of riding we were enchanted by the beauty of the land south of our property. Stream beds possessed clear, sweet-tasting water, and banks anchored by enormous cypress trees whose huge roots rose out of the ground as though they resented being covered by dirt. Majestic ancient oak trees stood alone in the middle of fields or off to the side in groups of ten to twenty.

Around the fire, we discussed the possibility of expanding further south. Unlike our wild and rocky Lost Maples Canyon, we could easily raise cattle on this land.

After six enjoyable days of riding, story-telling, and just responsibility-free living, we arrived in Austin just after midday. We headed over to the General Land Office where we found a new man behind the counter. I greeted him with, "Good afternoon, I am looking for the professor."

"He is no longer employed by the land office," barked the stranger. His comment was spewed out, not as information, but as a challenge. I was taken aback.

"I am sorry to hear Professor Eldridge departed. A while back I bought some land and just wanted to work with him to sharpen up the boundaries."

"We no longer sharpen up boundaries. What you bought is what you get," he practically spat out. I looked at Dennis and Darryl who looked equally stunned at this blatant hostility. Dismissing us with a wave of his hand, the new land manager pointed to the door.

In a state of confusion, we went down to the two banks so that Dennis could put his signature on the account in his name and on the joint account. Behind closed doors, each bank manager told us his tellers had been approached with a bribe to reveal how much money we had in the bank. They were not sure who was behind the bribes, but there were whispers it occurred at every bank in Austin.

Dennis and I just looked at one another. What in the world was going on?

Though thirsty, we decided to drop by Ranger Headquarters and thank them for saving our bacon before hitting any saloons. When we walked into the building, Captain Eldridge was standing at the door as though expecting us. "Come in gentlemen," he said and led us into his office.

Before I could even thank him for the Ranger's actions that saved the ranch and gold mine Captain Eldridge asked, "Did you run into Sam on the trail?"

Shaking my head no I said, "We did not run into him."

Captain Eldridge nodded thoughtfully. "Two days ago, I sent him down to warn you to come to Austin. The attack on the mule drivers and your ranch was too well organized for some loose outlaw outfit. I believe that even more now. Since the grab of your land with a gun failed, the fight has shifted to paper."

"Professor Eldridge at the land office was fired two weeks ago. A week after his firing, a banker who has only been in town six months came forward with a land deed to your mine. He claims the mine was bought with a Republic of Texas war voucher two years ago. He has filed suit to seize the mine."

I started laughing and the Ranger pulled back in confusion. "Sir, we built a decoy so that if someone tried to steal the mine they would steal a worthless hole in the ground."

Captain Eldridge did that thing where he stares at you for several minutes. He said, "Start from the beginning."

I told the story from start to finish and sat back with a self-satisfied grin at our cunning foresight. Captain Eldridge sat staring at me. After several moments he said, "The problem with your plan, is the banker has claimed not only the gold mine but all the gold you have mined so far.

Which means all your gold in the banks, as well as the land you bought with the gold."

A long period of staring followed this statement. When Captain Eldridge spoke again, it was slow and deliberate. "I hate outlaws. Using a gun to steal is bad enough. Using the law to steal is downright vile. This is what we are going to do, we are going to see Sam Houston. He was the first president of Texas and now represents the San Augustine district in the Texas House of Representatives.[1] Sam is a friend of mine."

We rode over to Sam Houston's office where I retold my story to the most famous man in Texas. General Houston laughed. He knew the judge who represented the Austin district to be an honest man and agreed to speak to him on our behalf.

Just like that, I was sitting in Judge Massey's office,[2] with the head of the Rangers on one side, and the former President of Texas on the other. I retold my story, and its end was met with a peal of laughter. "The solution is easy gentlemen. Men of honor and a mining expert must visit both mines and provide testimony to the value of the mines."

With a twinkle in his eye the judge said, "General, that would be you and the good Captain."

General Houston said, "I was hoping you would say that. I am sick to death of politics. A week away would do me good. How about you Captain Eldridge, can you spare some time on the trail?"

For the first time in our acquaintance, Captain Eldridge smiled, "Time I got back in the field. My men have been wondering if I have gone soft."

The judge continued, "I will try to delay the paperwork as long as possible. Rye, during your absence I will hire a good lawyer for you. Don Charanza knows all about land grants, the new Texas laws, and enjoys a good brawl. I will instruct him to investigate the land and Archives Office firings. I know you just got to town but leave immediately. If you are not here, they cannot serve you papers for the lawsuit."

Thanking all three gentlemen profusely, I jumped on my horse and rejoined Darryl and Dennis. "I will tell you on the trail. We have to get out of town, now."

Once we were several hours out of Austin we slowed down, and I recounted the incredible turn of events. Even in the retelling, it sounded so outrageous it sounded like a tall tale. General Sam Houston, the hero of

San Jacinto, the first president of Texas was coming to our ranch. I was excited to meet General Houston but disappointed at not seeing Tib during our trip to Austin.

NOTES

1. Ray Stephens, *Texas: A Historical Atlas* (Norman, OK: University of Oklahoma Press, 2010), 100. Stephen F. Austin (1793-1836) was the father of Texas, but Sam Houston (1793-1863) certainly took over that role after Austin's death in 1836. Sam Houston was Commander-in-Chief of the Texas Army when Santa Anna was defeated at San Jacinto in 1836. He served as the first (1836-1838) and third (1841-1844) President of the Republic of Texas, and a member of the Texas House of Representatives for the San Augustine district (1839-1841). After the annexation of Texas, Sam Houston served as a U.S. senator (1846-1859) and the seventh Governor of Texas (1859-1861). While Sam Houston was governor, a Texas political convention voted to secede on February 1, 1861. When Sam Houston refused to swear loyalty to the Confederacy he was replaced in office by Edward Clark in March 1861.

2. Forgive the personal indulgence. Massey was the last name of my maternal great-grandmother, Emma Massey before she married Robert Eldridge (all Texans). While in a confessional state, Dietrich is my maternal grandmother's name (also a Texan), and Eldridge is my maternal grandfather's name.

CHAPTER TWENTY-SEVEN

General Houston, the mining expert Mr. Stan Hetrick, and Captain Eldridge arrived at Lost Maples two days after our return. Fortunately, they arrived on the fourth of July, a day we had already planned on having a feast to celebrate the Independence Day of our big brother to the east. Kel had hunted that morning and a fresh deer was already cooking slowly over a pit as they rode up. Darryl had contributed eight quail that were laid out on a bed of coals and Dennis was frying up a mess of sunfish.

Introductions quickly swept through the crowd. Juan was hesitant at first, but the graciousness of our guests wiped out his fears. Both General Houston and Captain Eldridge commented it was a pleasure to meet Juan's delightful family. They congratulated Kel, Dennis, Heidi, and Consuela on their marriage, and wished them many children. General Houston picked up Kara and Teresa, alternately throwing them into the air.

Not one to waste time, General Houston asked to see the two mines. We walked to the first stone house built on the property and removed portions of the wood floor. I walked down the ladder first with a lit torch to make sure there were no rattlesnakes.

At the bottom of the ladder, I handed each person coming down a torch of their own and warned them to watch for rattlesnakes. I pointed to the dead miner and related the story of finding him with the paper in his hand. We walked down the mine shaft and they marveled at the thick gold veins in the cave walls.

Climbing out of the cave everyone was bedazzled by what they had witnessed. General Houston, Captain Eldridge, and Mr. Hetrick each stared into the small bag of gold-veined crystal I gave them as a souvenir of their visit.

When we came to the decoy mine I stopped outside the locked door and explained we not only salted the mine with gold, but with a barrel of rattlesnakes. The General shared my distaste for killing things unnecessarily. He recommended we repeat the trick of rigging long poles to catch the snakes and dropping them into a large barrel before we explored the mine.

From experience, I knew catching the snakes would take up much of the day. I recommended we start the next morning. We spent the night around a big fire where people feasted and told stories that became more and more outrageous as the night wore on. Years later the tall tales told by General Houston and Captain Eldridge turned out to be true. The world is a wonder.

During breakfast, there was a scratching at the door. I walked to the door but before opening it I turned to my guests and said, "Please don't reach for your weapons. We have a pet that is full-grown and spends most of her time away from home. She does return every couple of days to check-in."

I opened the door and Kit sauntered into the house. Now at eighteen months old, Kit was an impressive creature. The fact Kit had eaten well her whole life ensured she grew up healthy and maximized the growth she could attain. She was seven-foot-long and weighed one hundred and eighty pounds, more than most full-grown male cats. Her tawny coat glowed with health and had none of the scars and torn spots from a life of fighting to survive in the wild. Kit walked up to the fire and sat, waiting for someone to serve her what they were eating.

Our guests stared from one to the other. Finally, General Houston grinned mischievously and asked, "Would you be insulted if I repeated the story of meeting your cat and maybe added a bit to spice up the telling?" We all laughed, looking forward to hearing whatever wild tale General Houston decided to spin.

After breakfast, General Houston, Captain Eldridge, Mr. Hetrick, Kel, Dennis, and Darryl stood ready with their long poles and leather loops as I unlocked the decoy mine door. The big door swung open and two rattlesnakes at the threshold immediately coiled up and began to rattle.

With a whoop, General Houston dropped his hoop over the head of one snake, as Kel did so with the other. The snakes were quickly dropped into the barrel as we lit torches on the walls with every piece of ground we gained.

We spent the morning capturing the snakes without incidence. I pointed out fewer snakes were in the cave than I remembered. Mr. Hetrick commented, "If there is not a handy supply of mice, rats, bats, or frogs, the snakes probably are eating one another."

Mr. Hetrick examined every foot of the mine. After careful deliberation, he said, "There is no doubt this mine never produced gold."

Grinning, General Houston asked, "If our examination of the mine is completed, may I have the honor of rolling the snake barrel back into the mine?"

"Sure," we responded in unison. What else could we have said?

With a mighty shove, the barrel rolled down the mine and stopped, with the lid still in place. "Hm," everyone mumbled. With a little bit of trepidation, we walked down the shaft and examined the barrel from a distance. The barrel remained intact and the lid still firmly affixed.

Suggestions filled the air, "We can stand the barrel up." "Swing an ax and knock the lid off." "Roll it again."

Much discussion followed and it was decided the safest approach would be to blow a hole in the top of the barrel with a shotgun. The snakes could just crawl out of the barrel on their own. Kel grabbed a Colt shotgun and standing as close to the barrel as possible, blew a melon-sized hole in the top of the barrel which tipped over on its side as snakes poured out of the hole. We watched in fascination as the snakes slithered out of the barrel and coiled up on the cave floor rattling. With a shiver, we closed and locked the mine doors, grown men grinning like naughty children.

We returned to the house where each of our three guests immediately wrote out statements regarding the two mines. In the morning, everyone decided that for legal reasons, Kel, Dennis, Darryl, and I, would have to accompany our guests back to Austin. Juan agreed that during our absence, he and his family would move into the original stone house with Heidi and Kara, which was the most defensible.

CHAPTER TWENTY-EIGHT

On the outskirts of Austin, General Houston, Captain Eldridge, and Mr. Hetrick separated from us, and one another, so that no one saw us together. Our first stop was at the law office of Mr. Don Charanza, the lawyer the judge arranged to represent us.

Opening the door to Mr. Charanza's opulent office, we were greeted by a distinguished gray-haired gentleman who oozed confidence and intelligence. The lawyer stepped out from behind his desk and said, "Thank you for hiring me. This is going to be a wonderful trial, the talk of Austin for years to come. I have taken the liberty of hiring as co-counsel Mr. Voelkel, the attorney who helped you on one of your previous visits to Austin."

Kel, Darryl, and I walked out of his office feeling confident. With a little swagger, I suggested a quick visit to the mercantile. Stopping outside the mercantile door, I suggested they wait outside while I visited Tib. When I walked in, Tib froze in place. She turned her back and stalked out of the room. Tib disappeared and her father entered from the back storeroom and stared frostily at me.

I was taken aback by her rejection and the hostility of her father. Standing there dumbly, unsure of what to do, I stumbled to the door and stepped outside with my heart ripped apart.

Prepared to josh me about Tib, Darryl and Dennis stopped mid-sentence at the pale look on my face. "Tib turned her back on me and her father is angry with me."

Alarmed, Darryl asked, "Did you molest her when she was at the house?"

"No, of course not. I would never do something like that," I practically yelled.

"Calm down, lower your voice," Dennis said.

The sparkle and lightness I felt just minutes ago evaporated, leaving behind a pain-ravaged grey veil. Tib wanted nothing to do with me.

Dazed, I stumbled to the hotel where we registered as guests for a week. I was unsure how long the trial would last, but now, to me, any amount of time in Austin would be intolerable.

A clerk from the court came to the hotel that evening and presented us with papers indicating the trial would start the next day. We ate our meals in the hotel and stayed in our rooms. A Ranger was stationed downstairs in the lobby. A rumor ran through Austin that there was a bounty on each of our heads.

The trial started in the morning with the banker Randolph Lincrest on the stand. In his expensive suit, Mr. Lincrest pompously described how he took over the failing Charlton Bank six months previously and renamed it Lincrest National. Upon purchasing the bank, he described slowly working his way through the bank's documents. In doing so, Mr. Lincrest discovered the bank had repossessed a piece of land from a customer, Jeremiah Friedricks who defaulted on a loan. The land was originally deeded to the bank's customer in 1837 with a Texas Revolution land voucher for his service at San Jacinto. The land had been repossessed in 1838 and misfiled. Only recently had the defaulted loan been discovered. When Mr. Lincrest went to the land office to determine where the land was located, he was surprised to find the land was in Lost Maples exactly where the gold mine was located.

Banker Lincrest's testimony was followed by the snarling land manager, Mr. Rupert Mandible, who confirmed the banker's testimony. "The land is a narrow parcel that starts south of the mine, encompasses the mine, and stops just short of the homestead property line of Mr. Ricky Lee Campise, the cowboy known as Rye," he added with a sneer.

The last person to testify was the newly appointed manager of the Texas Archives Office, Mr. Simon Nater. He confirmed there was a recorded deed in the land office that had been on file since 1837 for the property later discovered to be the Rattlesnake Gold Mine.

Adjourning the court for the day, Judge Massey instructed all the witnesses to return the next day in case additional testimony was required. Dismissively glancing at Rye, the haughty banker Lincrest sauntered out of the courtroom. His demeanor conveyed that as far as he was concerned, the trial was over.

On the second day of the trial, our lawyer Don Charanza stood up and said, "Your honor, this court seeks to discover two truths. Banker Lincrest contends the gold possessed by my client is owned by his bank because the gold came from the mine banker Lincrest claims to own. The first truth we must ascertain is the exact location from which the gold was mined. Secondly, we must discover the truth of who owns the gold the mine produced."

"My first witness is Mr. Stan Hetrick, an expert with the Texas Coal and Mine Department."

Mr. Hetrick was sworn in and said, "Your honor I have examined the land claimed by Mr. Lincrest and I can guarantee you no gold was ever extracted from that mine. The topography of the land is inconsistent with gold. In the mine itself, only rock and dirt have been removed and that is all that will ever come out of that hole. Without question, the gold was extracted from a different location."

My lawyer smiled knowingly at the judge and jury before calling up Captain Eldridge. Don Charanza laid out a flattering rendition of the Ranger's long history of service to Texas and unassailable integrity. Bowing, Don Charanza said, "Captain Eldridge, in your own words please describe your recent trip to Lost Maples."

For the next hour, Captain Eldridge detailed how he accompanied Mr. Hetrick through the mine claimed by banker Lincrest. He concluded his testimony by stating, "It is my belief the gold came from a different mine from that claimed by Mr. Lincrest. I have examined that second mine and like Mr. Hetrick believe the second mine is the source of the gold."

The courtroom was already reeling when Don Charanza theatrically boomed, "General Houston please take the stand."

Jumping to their feet, the packed audience applauded as General Houston slowly strode into the room. The hero of San Jacinto swung his hat in a wide circle and bowed in acknowledgment to the adoring crowd. General Houston repeated much of the same information as that shared by Captain Eldridge. The eloquent General's description of accompanying Mr. Hetrick and Captain Eldridge through the two mines was performed with such color and drama that the entire room sat spellbound.

When Sam Houston stepped down the judge declared, "It is clear the gold did not originate from the mine claimed by banker Lincrest. The claim against the gold in the banks and all purchases made with said gold is denied. The owners of the currently processed gold are Rye Campise and his associates."

While Sam Houston was sitting down in the front row, Don Charanza called up Professor Eldridge, the previous General Land Office manager. After being sworn in, Professor Eldridge said, "I was approached by a member of the staff of Mirabeau Lamar, the second and current president of the Republic of Texas. This man informed me I was to accept a false land document and assert it had been on file for years. I refused. The next day I was fired."

The new land manager who had been sitting in the audience got up to leave, but a Ranger put a hand on his shoulder. Pointing to the man, the judge said, "Please return to the stand, I suspect you may want to amend your testimony from yesterday."

Visibly shaking, Mr. Mandible returned to the witness chair and repeated his false story from yesterday. Don Charanza fired one question after another about how the new land manager obtained his position and the timing of the land claim. Mr. Mandible grew increasingly confused and his answers began to contradict themselves.

Angrily snapping his gavel, Judge Massey yelled, "Ranger, arrest this man for perjury." The shaking man was jerked off the stand as irons were placed on his hands and feet in front of the clamoring courtroom.

"The defense would like to call Mr. Lazaro Duremdes, the prior manager of the Texas Archives Office. Mr. Duremdes, please tell us how you came to lose your job?"

"I was approached by a member of the staff of Mirabeau Lamar. This man informed me I was to accept a false land document and assert it had been on file for years. I refused. The next day I was fired."

The current Texas Archives Office manager was trying to edge out the back door when a Ranger grabbed him by the collar and dragged him to the witness stand. With a fierce tone, Judge Massey asked, "Mr. Nater, you now face a year in jail for perjury. Do you wish to amend your testimony?"

Looking at the floor, Mr. Nater squeaked out, "I was told I would be appointed head of the Archives Office and given a bonus if I would support the claim of Mr. Lincrest."

With contempt, the judge looked at Mr. Nater and said, "You are dismissed. Ranger, please take custody of Mr. Nater. He will be charged with perjury for his previous false statements."

At this point, Sam Houston stood up and said, "Your honor, I know it is somewhat irregular, but would you call me back to the stand?"

Upon returning to the stand, General Houston said, "If it would please the court, I would like to point out I spent a little time at San Jacinto." The audience laughed loudly. "I looked every man in the eye before the battle and shook every hero's hand after our victory even though I was stretched out on the ground with a painful leg wound." General Houston reached down and rubbed his leg as the audience hushed into silence.

"I can tell you no man named Jeremiah Friedricks ever served under my command at San Jacinto. To claim so is treasonous, and an insult to every man who served there that day."

Pointing to banker Lincrest, General Houston said, "You sir, are a thief and a traitor to the Republic of Texas. In the sacred name of San Jacinto, you perpetrated fraud. I want the name of the man on Lamar's staff that helped you execute these sordid crimes. I will call a special session of the House to investigate these crimes to ensure you all go to jail and these decent men get their jobs back."

Staring at the banker and his two fellow conspirators, General Houston said, "Unlike you, these four gentlemen are Texas heroes. Not only did they fight for the Republic, but when they mined their gold, they filed a legal document with their lawyer to start a fund to support injured soldiers of the Texas Revolution and their families. You, sir, are stealing from our nation, its heroes, and their families."

The crowd erupted in boos. Yells of "lynch them" filled the courtroom. If the Rangers had not been present, the banker and his fellow crooks would have found themselves dangling on the end of a rope.

Barely audible over the cheers and shouts, the judge said, "I find the gold and the land belongs to Mr. Campise and his associates. Case dismissed. Ranger, arrest Mr. Lincrest and place him in a cell along with his two crooked companions."

Men and women congregated around General Houston, eager to be able to say they touched his coat or shook his hand. Eventually, the courtroom began to clear as Kel, Darryl, Dennis, and I sat back in our chairs and just stared at the room in wonder. I turned in my chair to look at the back of the room and saw Tib standing near the door.

After our last meeting, I was unsure whether to approach Tib. I watched her, but she refused to make eye contact with me. Kel, now that he had a woman of his own, seemed much more comfortable with women. He walked back to Tib, leaned in, and whispered something in her ear. Tib burst into tears and ran from the room.

I walked over to Kel and asked, "What in the world did you tell her?"

Kel shrugged and said, "I told Tib I wished she would visit Lost Maples to meet my wife Consuela."

He and I looked at each other and shook our heads. I turned back and shook hands with our two lawyers Don Charanza and Shanty Voelkel who chuckled, "This is the most fun we have had in a long time."

Sam Houston said something along the same lines. "I don't know why I became a politician. I liked my old life of riding the trail and leading an army more than I like signing papers and listening to mutton heads drone on."

Nodding with respect I said, "That is some feat to remember the name of every man to serve under your command."

Sam Houston smiled and with a twinkle in his eye said, "Do I?"

Everyone laughed. We thanked General Houston and encouraged him to visit us any time. We shook hands with Captain Eldridge and told him his Rangers were welcome at Lost Maples for a meal, a roof over their heads, and a fresh horse at any time of day or night.

The boys would not let me leave town without seeing Tib again. They practically pushed me onto my horse. Grabbing my horse's reins, they started pulling my horse towards the mercantile. Halfway there, I saw Mr. O'Shay stumbling up the street. He rushed into the road and grabbed the reins to stop my horse. The storekeeper's face was absent any hostility and he looked stricken. "I am sorry, so very sorry. Tib is in the back room of the mercantile, you must see her."

Continuing our journey to the mercantile, the boys shoved me through the door. With dread, I walked into the empty store. Tib was nowhere to be seen, so I went into the stock room. In the dim light, a mound of red hair was hunched behind a crate sobbing.

I did not know what to do so I just squatted down on my knees and placed a hand on Tib's shoulder. Tears streaming from her eyes, Tib pounced on me and drove me to the floor. Wrapping her arms around me, in between sobs Tib wailed, "One of the Rangers told me you married a woman named Consuela. I did not know it was Kel. They told me it was you."

THE END

BIBLIOGRAPHY

BOOKS

Hart, Charles, Tam Garland, Catherine Barr, Bruce Carpenter, and John Reagor. *Toxic Plants of Texas: Integrated Management Services to Prevent Livestock Losses.* Texas AgriLife Extension Service, 2003.

Hunter, Marvin J. *The Boy Captives.* San Angelo, TX: Anchor Publishing Co, (1927) 1995. Citations refer to the seventh reprint in 1995.

Jenkins, John Holmes III, ed. *Recollections of Early Texas: The Memoirs of John Holland Jenkins.* Austin, TX: University of Texas Press, (1958) 1975. Citations refer to the fourth reprint in 1975.

Loflin, Brian and Loflin, Shirley. *Grasses of the Texas Hill Country.* College Station, TX: Texas A&M University Press, 2006.

Matthews, Rupert. *The Illustrated Encyclopedia of Small Arms: From Hand Cannons to Automatic Weapons.* San Diego, CA: Thunder Bay Press, 2014.

Stephens, Ray. *Texas: A Historical Atlas.* Norman, OK: University of Oklahoma Press, 2010.

Turner, Matt. *Remarkable Plants of Texas.* Austin, TX: University of Texas Press, 2009.

Walton, Greg, ed. *Bear Meat 'n' Honey: An Oral History of the Sabinal Canyon.* Vol 1. Austin, TX: Acorn Press, 1990.

Zesch, Scott. *Captured: A True Story of Abduction by Indians on the Texas Frontier.* New York: St. Martin's Press, 2004.

ONLINE

FindLaw. "Texas Homestead Law Overview." Accessed May 3, 2018.
https://statelaws.findlaw.com/texas-law/texas-homestead-law-
overview.html.

Handbook of Texas Online. Cutrer, Thomas W. "McCullough,
Benjamin." Accessed May 7, 2020.
https://www.tshaonline.org/handbook/online/articles/fmc34.

Handbook of Texas Online. Cutrer, Thomas W. "Smith, Erastus (Deaf)."
Accessed May 7, 2020.
https://www.tshaonline.org/handbook/online/articles/fsm10.

Handbook of Texas Online. Dobie, Frank J. "Wallace, William Anderson
(Big Foot)." Accessed May 7, 2020.
https://www.tshaonline.org/handbook/online/articles/fwa36.

Handbook of Texas Online. Johnson, John G. "Capitals." Accessed May
10, 2018.
https://www.tshaonline.org/handbook/online/articles/mzc01.

Handbook of Texas Online. Lack, Paul D. "Revolutionary Army."
Accessed March 11, 2020,
https://tshaonline.org/handbook/online/articles/qjr03.

Handbook of Texas Online. Roell, Craig H. "Linnville Raid of 1840."
Accessed May 14, 2018.
https://tshaonline.org/handbook/online/articles/btl01.

Handbook of Texas Online. Williamson, William R. "Bowie Knife."
Accessed May 5, 2020.
https://tshaonline.org/handbook/online/articles/lnb01.

Handbook of Texas Online. Williamson, William. R. "James Bowie."
Accessed May 3, 2020.
https://tshaonline.org/handbook/online/articles/fb045.

Hawk Migration Association of North America. "New to Hawk
Watching?" Accessed April 30, 2020. www.hmana.org.

Hummingbird Central. "Spring 2020 Hummingbird Migration Map and
Sightings." Accessed April 28, 2020,
https://www.hummingbirdcentral.com.

Military Factory. "Baker Rifle." Accessed April 8, 2018.
https://www.militaryfactory.com/smallarms/detail.asp?smallarms_id
=925.

Military Factory. "Henry Model 1813." Accessed April 14, 2018.
https://www.militaryfactory.com/smallarms/detail.asp?smallarms_id
=804#performance.

Military Factory. "Johnson Model 1836." Accessed April 14, 2018.
https://www.militaryfactory.com/smallarms/detail.asp?smallarms_id
=31.

Sons of the DeWitt Colony. Bryant, John. "The Small Arms and Weapons
of the Alamo Defenders." Accessed 3 April 2018.
http://www.sonsofdewittcolony.org/adp/history/1836/the_battle/the
_weapons/small_arms.html.

Taylor, Lonn. "Remember the Long Rifle." *Texas Monthly* (March 2015).
https://www.texasmonthly.com/the-culture/remember-the-long-
rifle/.

Texas Butterfly Ranch (March 17, 2020). Maeckle, Monika. "Monarch
Butterfly Numbers Drop As Spring Migration Begins."
https://texasbutterflyranch.com.

Texas Department of Public Safety. "Texas Rangers Historical Development." Accessed April 28, 2020. https://www.dps.texas.gov/TexasRangers/HistoricalDevelopment.thm.

Texas General Land Office. "Categories of Land Grants." Accessed April 5, 2018. www.glo.texas.gov/history/archives/forms/files/glo-headright-military-land-grants.pdf.

Texas Hill Country. Tackitt, Llyod. "The Billion Dollar Lost Mine of the Hill Country." Accessed May 3, 2020. https://texashillcountry.com/billion-dollar-lost-silver-mine-hill-country/.

Travis Audubon. Spencer, Jim. "What to Watch for in September: High-Flyers." Accessed May 2, 2020. https://travisaudubon.org/uncategorized/September-bird-forecast-high-flyers.

Wikipedia. "Battle of Plum Creek." Accessed April 28, 2020. https://en.wikipedia.org/wiki/Battle_of_Plum_Creek.

Wikipedia. "Brown Bess." Accessed February 10, 2018. https://en.wikipedia.org/wiki/Brown_Bess.

Wikipedia. "Colt Paterson." Accessed April 10, 2018. https://en.wikipedia.org/wiki/Colt_Paterson.

Wikipedia. "Council House Fight." Accessed April 10, 2018. https://en.wikipedia.org/wiki/Council_House_Fight.

Wikipedia. "Henry Lee lll." Accessed June 7, 2018. https://en.wikipedia.org/wiki/Henry_Lee_lll.

Wikipedia. "Old Three Hundred." Accessed April 16, 2018. https://en.wikipedia.org/wiki/Old_Three_Hundred.

Wikipedia. "Percussion Cap." Accessed April 18, 2018. https://en.m.wikipedia.org/wiki/Percussion_Cap.

Wikipedia. "Ranger Division." Accessed May 4, 2018. https://en.wikipedia.org/wiki/Texas_Ranger_Division.

Wikipedia. "Republic of Texas." Accessed April 24, 2021. https://en.wikipedia.org/wiki/Republic_of_Texas.

CHARACTERS

Bartlet — Kel's friend, accompanied Kel while paying for land vouchers

Ben McCullough — Benjamin McCullough, famous Texas Ranger

Ben Highsmith — Benjamin Franklin Highsmith, famous Texas Ranger

Big Foot Wallace — William Anderson Wallace, famous Texas Ranger

Captain Jim Eldridge — Head of Texas Rangers

Consuela — Married Kel

Dan — Dead miner 1834

Darryl — Rye's brother

Deaf Smith — Erastus Smith, famous Texas Ranger

Dennis — Rye's cousin

Don Charanza — Lawyer referred by Sam Houston

Gebert and Hobart — Mule wagon drivers tasked by Mr. O'Shay with protecting Tib

Heidi — Seventeen-year-old woman rescued when Kara was kidnapped

Javier — Consuela's younger brother

Jeremiah Friedricks — San Jacinto veteran alleged to have defaulted on a gold mine loan

Jimmy — Uncle who taught Rye how to skin an animal

Juan — Consuela's father, horse wrangler

Judge Massey — Austin judge presiding at Rye's mine ownership trial

Kara — Karankawa child adopted by Rye, Kel, Darryl, and Dennis

Kel — Rye's best friend

Kit — Cougar

Lazaro Duremdes — Republic of Texas Records Archives Manager

Moss — Hermit who shot Rye and died of rattlesnake bites

Randolph Lincrest — Crooked banker

Rye — Main character who discovers gold

Rupert Mandible — Crooked General Land Office Manager

Sam — Texas Ranger assigned to guard Rye's gold wagon

Sarah McCullough — Young woman killed by Comanche

Simon Nater — Crooked Republic of Texas Archives Manager

Stan Hetrick — Mining expert

Sam Houston — First President of Texas

Shanty Voelkel — Lawyer recommended by Ranger Sam

TIMELINE

1810 — Ferdinand VII is the king of Spain

16 Sep 1810 — Date Mexico began its struggle for independence from Spain. Father Miguel Hidalgo y Costilla declared Mexico's independence from Spain in the town of Dolores.

Jan 1817 — Rye and Kel born

Dec 1817 — Dennis born

Jul 1819 — Darryl born

24 Aug 1821 — Spain grants Mexico's Independence

1824-1828 — Stephen Fuller Austin "Father of Texas" led the second colonization of Texas. He brought 297 families to Texas. Defeated in his bid for Texas Presidency, Austin served as Secretary of State until he died in 1836.

1824 — Sam the Texas Ranger born

1828 — Rye and Kel become neighbors when they are ten years old

1834 — Deceased miner's original discovery of Rattlesnake Gold Mine

Oct 1835 - Apr 1836 — War of Texas Independence

9-10 Oct 1835 — Battle of Goliad

12 Oct-11 Dec 1835 — Siege of Bexar

23 Feb-6 Mar 1836 — Alamo (estimated 183 to 200 defenders died)

27 Mar 1836 — Goliad Massacre (four hundred Texans died)

21 Apr 1836 — Battle of San Jacinto (Rye and Kel are nineteen, Dennis is eighteen, Darryl is seventeen)

27 Dec 1836 — Stephen F. Austin died of pneumonia at the age of forty-three

1836 — Rye departs Texas (Rye is nineteen)

1837 — Waterloo village founded on banks of Colorado River

27 Nov 1838-9 Mar 1839 — The Pastry War: Fight between Mexico and France

1839 — Revised Colt Paterson, cylinder removed without disassembly

1839 — President Lamar was elected second President of Texas. Texas Congress appoints a capital site selection committee. Austin is founded on the site of the Waterloo area with a purchase of 7,035 acres.

Mar 1839 — Austin officially chartered as the capital of Texas

Oct 1839 — Government of Texas moves to Austin (Jan 1840 population 839)

Dec 1839 — Rye returns to Texas (Rye is twenty-two)

8 Dec 1839 — Rye finds gold

18 Dec 1839 — Rye shoots three outlaws outside Austin

19 Dec 1839 — Rye visits Texas Rangers Headquarters in Austin to explain dead outlaws. Buys land and sends a coded message for Kel, Darryl, and Dennis. Meets Tib at mercantile, trades guns and horses for a wagon.

19-31 Dec 1839 — Rye travels from Austin to Lost Maples

1 Jan 1840 — Rye arrives at Lost Maples (twenty-three years old)

10 Jan 1840 — Comanche ask Texans for meeting to discuss peace

Mid-Mar 1840 — Rye finds two-month-old cougar kitten

19 Mar 1840 — Council House peace meeting turns into Council House Massacre

End-Apr 1840 — Two outlaws visit the ranch

End-Apr 1840 — Kel (twenty-three), Darryl (twenty-one), Dennis (twenty-two) arrive

Mid-May 1840 — Karankawa at seep, camp on the ranch

14 Jun 1840 — Comanche attack the Karankawa camp and Kara is the only survivor. Build a decoy mine.

6 Aug 1840 — Chief Buffalo Hump attacks Victoria

8 Aug 1840 — Chief Buffalo Hump attacks Linnville

12 Aug 1840 — Battle of Plum Creek

Mid-Dec 1840 — Kara is kidnapped by Comanche. Rye, Darryl, Kel, and Dennis rescue Kara and Heidi.

18 Jan 1841 — Kel and Darryl depart to Waller to pay for land vouchers

21 Jan 1841 — Rye departs to Austin driving a wagon filled with gold. Informs Captain Eldridge about outlaws, Indian captives, and gold.

5 Feb 1841 — Rye, Kel, and Darryl meet in Austin and open bank accounts. Rye sees Tib again, buys four wagons and five wagons of merchandise.

9 Feb 1841 — Kit kills two outlaws, Dennis kills two outlaws

10 Feb 1841 — Rye, Kel, and Darryl return to Lost Maples from Austin

22 Feb 1841 — Tib and wagons arrive at Lost Maples

1 Mar 1841 — Ranch attacked by thirty-five outlaws. Twenty-one outlaws were shot (two wounded, nineteen dead).

8 Mar 1841 — Rangers Big Foot Wallace, Ben Highsmith, Ben McCullough, and Sam kill fifteen outlaws. Tib departs with the Rangers.

25 Apr 1841 — Mexican family hired as Lost Maples hands

25 May 1841 — Kel, Darryl, Rye, and Juan depart for San Antonio. Kel steals a priest and marries Consuela. Dennis marries Heidi.

25 Jun 1841 — Captain Eldridge tells Rye of the attempt to steal his mine. Rye meets Judge Massey and General Houston.

4 Jul 1841 — Sam Houston, Captain Eldridge, and Stan Hetrick visit Lost Maples Ranch

15 Jul 1841 — Trial in Austin over Rattlesnake Gold Mine

ABOUT THE AUTHOR

Rick Campise is a fifth generation Texan born in Houston, Texas. He is a pediatric psychologist who received his Ph.D. from the University of Kansas and completed a postdoctoral fellowship in pediatric psychology at Harvard.

In 2015, Dr. Campise retired after twenty-eight years of service as a Colonel in the United States Air Force.

With his wife, Tib, Col (r) Campise now spends his time hiking, reading, and pursuing his love of Texas history.

NOTE FROM THE AUTHOR

Word-of-mouth is crucial for any author to succeed. If you enjoyed *Lost Maples*, please leave a review online—anywhere you are able. Even if it's just a sentence or two. It would make all the difference and would be very much appreciated.

Thanks!
Rick L. Campise

We hope you enjoyed reading this title from:

BLACK ROSE
writing™

www.blackrosewriting.com

Subscribe to our mailing list – *The Rosevine* – and receive
FREE books, daily deals, and stay current with news about
upcoming releases and our hottest authors.
Scan the QR code below to sign up.

Already a subscriber? Please accept a sincere thank you for
being a fan of Black Rose Writing authors.

View other Black Rose Writing titles at
www.blackrosewriting.com/books and use promo code
PRINT to receive a **20% discount** when purchasing.